CW01086220

Snuggie Bobo grew up in the rural Midwest, but soon became enticed with running the streets of the hood. It became an area to be conquered by all means necessary! This, of course, led to a long stay in 'upstate' maximum security correctional college nicknamed 'Gladiator School'. It was the school of hard knocks where men left better criminals than they entered. In the process of trying to omit the truth of the past years' regrets, Snuggie became educated, going as far as obtaining a PhD with the hopes to rejoin society. Unfortunately, society tends to look down upon street hoods and ex-felons! Now, Snuggie lives in Chicagoland spinning tales based on this lived history to bring the reader into his world. Sean Jr. was one of the people in this world. He was a gay brother, who lost his father to crack. His father was dealing with their family problem. Sean's mother abused him due to his forbidden illness: lusting for men. Snuggie knew Sean since he was knee-high to a grasshopper and years later took him in. He was his mentor. These are tales out of Sean and Snuggie's life.

Author Contact: snuggie.bobo.tale@gmail.com

To all the players which I have met; straight or gay, I hope you have found your personal peace and peace with the world.

Snuggie Bobo

STORY 1: THE DELIGHTS OF SEAN JR.

Gay Urban Stories of a Player's Lust

AUSTIN MACAULEY PUBLISHERS™

LONDON • CAMBRIDGE • NEW YORK • SHARJAH

Ordering Information
Quantity sales: Special discounts are available on quantity purchases by corporations, associations, and others. For details, contact the publisher at the address below.

Publisher's Cataloging-in-Publication data
Bobo, Snuggie
Story 1: The Delights of Sean Jr.

Library of Congress Control Number: 2024902119

ISBN 9798889102281 (Paperback)
ISBN 9798889102298 (Hardback)
ISBN 9798889102311 (ePub e-book)
ISBN 9798889102304 (Audiobook)

www.austinmacauley.com/us

First Published 2024
Austin Macauley Publishers LLC
40 Wall Street, 33rd Floor, Suite 3302
New York, NY 10005
USA

mail-usa@austinmacauley.com
+1 (646) 5125767

Table of Contents

Introduction   9

1. The Bar Scene   10

2. Supper with Sis   31

3. Unck Got Even   57

4. County Jail Madness   62

5. Playing with Doctor Zak   82

6. Getting to Know Friends of a Feather   100

7. Gettin Lucky in County   111

8. Trouble Comes in County   125

9. Released   133

10. Thay and Sean   140

11. Dewayne and Tone   148

12. Breakfast with the Parents   163

13. Or, Did the Story Stop?   169

Introduction

So the tale begins with Sean Jr. and Uncle Whitey or 'Unck' as Sean calls him. The crossroad of two men had met. Their separate lives were now changed and a new timeline started for both. The stories of a player's lust begins.

1. The Bar Scene

The college hangout was busting with action. Sean and Zak sat on bar stools around a small table for four. The music was a little slower where they sat, but the dance hall connected to it was popping. Unknown to Sean, Zak started to have thoughts about getting busy right there with him. Zak now and then glanced at Sean's pants. He knew he was wearing his sports cup. He notice sometimes his penis would swell. Sean was a little different.

* * *

To understand Sean was to know him; he was my boy. After a bad childhood, I took him in as my own. My women supported the idea. Sean and I came from two different cultures: two different walks of life.

I was from European descent. He was not. I knew him as a young lad which grew into a man. I was the 'old guy' that barely hit five-foot-eleven. I had blond hair. I knew the younger Sean thought I lived a mysterious, almost mystical life. However, these were childhood thoughts. As his family life changed for the worst I looked out for him. After he ran away, he eventually looked for me.

Sean was African-American. He stood six-foot-five tall, or so, and weighed around 230 pounds. Sean was chiseled from the weight room and playing ball. He was pretty much all muscle. Sean stayed in shape; he still had his twenty-seven-inch waist. God blessed him with a beautiful body. He was a beast. As a brother, he was properly proportioned. He knew he was hung.

While staying at my place, one day I knocked on the bathroom door. "Sean, I do have to go to work." I wanted to clean up, too. I watched him come out wearing nothing. He stood with a half erection. Our eyes met. "Hey, can I shower?"

I never had any desires for a man. Yet, I knew he liked men. It was a tough one to understand. To him a natural erection was nothing to be embarrassed about or hide. While at home with me, he sometimes acted like he was still in a men's locker room. I grew up differently. However, this was now my boy.

"Okay, Unck, I am done," Sean smiled. "Sorry, Unck, things got hard." He grabbed a towel to put it around his waist.

"Thank you!" He was just being natural. He told me sometimes when alone, he would pull on himself many times. As gay man, he thought it was natural. Oddly, we did have a very open honest relationship with each other; sometimes I thought he was too open and honest! He explained to me about his mother who thought his lifestyle was wrong. Basically, she wanted to cut them two things off between his legs.

"Unck, I will go to my bedroom to finish dressing."

Things like this opened my eyes to a gay man. As a mentor, I did not want him to send the wrong message to people. His height sometimes scared people. He was like a tower. Many others thought he was a basketball star. His dress wear was sometimes a little snug. He had a great deal of frontage and backside exposed. He dressed how he did.

He was not a bad kid, it was the culture he grew in. Other times he sagged. Many people would see him in lose clothes. They thought he was a thug. He was just a black man trying to blend.

Some took his gayness to be a weakness. As a gay man he was not weak. This brought some fights. With me and my girl, we worked with it. It was difficult sometimes to see him go through these challenges.

Yet, there is more. Sean's mama told him throughout his young life that his groin was the family's curse. She used it against him since he was her only boy. She could not deal with his gayness. I could never understand how a mother could reject a child because of his sexual differences. All children need love. She used what God gave him as a tool to hate him.

She rejected him. How do I say it? She rejected him because of his sexuality. Who am I to judge him like she did? It was Sean.

* * *

As Sean sat on the edge of the bar stool, anyone could see a well-rounded groin hanging in his thin khakis. He liked playing with his nuts even when he talked. If his sexual tension was aroused, his swipe would sometimes lengthen. With a thinner waist, he had a great deal of meat to store inconspicuously behind a zipper!

* * *

To help this he wore sexy athletic cups to hold it all in. This restricted movement. I was shopping with him one day where he went into the bathroom with another man. As we met up to checkout, he apparently removed his cup. Anyone could see it.

Truth be told, he was a beautiful man. Sean did not try to brag about his size. It was just there, he was born with it. The thug in him did not care about hiding it. He wanted to show it. If he got aroused while wearing boxers, he would sometimes get a little embarrassed if it lengthen. Yet, he liked it.

On dates in public places, he wore one of his designer cups. The road he was on was going two different directions. He liked to pick up men. Sometimes he scratched his nut and pulled his swipe out of the cup to let it hang. Other times he tried to hide it. It was Sean.

As his Unck, he told me I did not understand. I wanted him to become something greater. If he got an erection sometimes, I knew as a young man it would happen; the male body does get sexually excited. He was at his peck. He was not trying to show it to the world, but in his words: "How do I hide thirteen inches? Unck, I'm gay." He thought to himself, *It is a great deal to hide. Wow, now Unck is on me!*

His new friend Zak was shorter: five foot ten and a little stocky. Zak's stockiness brought them together. "I like them like that," Sean told me. When they were in my house, I could see that they liked each other. They both enjoyed playing ball together. Zak physically was a thick dick brother with a smaller penis head. Yes, Sean shared it with me. If it was hard, it was six inches. His nuts were a little larger than average. Zak had that beautiful G-Q look which some men are blessed with. Zak always dressed nicely.

Sometimes it was difficult for Sean. I could see he and Zak were raised differently. When they were over sometimes, I did my best to help keep the peace. However, it did seem those two really did like each other.

As I mentioned, Zak's family raised him differently. According to Sean, Zak's mother always told him to wear briefs so people would not get the wrong idea. He had to wear tight briefs. Boxers were not for him. If a male showed a swelling in his pants, a person might get the wrong idea. He was not allowed to sag like Sean did. Zak was taught to wear slacks with a waist and inseam which correctly fit.

Sometimes, if his mother thought the clothes he wore exposed too much visually around his groin, she would have him go to his room to change. When he got older, adolescence took over so he would ejaculate. He would stand in front of his closet door mirror and pull his penis as fast as he could to ejaculate. He loved watching his creamy stuff flow out of his body. It felt so great.

When he was done, he would dispose of the cloth. He could not tell his loving parents. He went through so many wash cloths and socks, he started buying them with his allowance. He thought if he jagged this would help keep his penis less obvious. Yet, he needed to have sex.

If he saw a male he lusted for, he would get an uncontrollable erection at the wrong time. If in public or by his parents, he would sit straighter and force his swipe between his legs. Sometimes, he would pass juices in his pants. He noticed he got wet. All young men know those things happen!

What a pair they made.

* * *

The bar steward approached the table, "How are you gentlemen doing?"

They both sat enjoying the beginning of the evening. They both would touch each other. Sean had a 40 oz. in front of him and Zak was drinking a diet Pepsi. Before Sean came to the bar, Zak used some of them chemicals. Zak was perfect picture, Sean had the look of a thug. Today he dressed to prepare for an erection. If he sagged, no one could see it. They both were very horny. Their penises were swelling. Sean now and then touched his nuts.

"I could use another diet Pepsi; thank you," Zak replied. Zak's mother always taught him to be polite. He was also sometimes compelled to adjust his clothes so they were aligned. He did not want a half hard swipe to show; that would be rude! His mother told him when in public he should not let anyone see his penis pressing on his pants. Hence, the tight briefs.

"Which one of you is Sean?" She had two glasses on her tray.

"Me." Sean smiled. He felt his swipe lengthen. He was around Zak.

"So, you must be Zak?"

"Yes." Zak smiled, while feeling the sensation grow in his pants. He was around Sean.

They both were trying to hook up for sex. However, neither wanted to say it. Yet, they both knew each other was gay. They both shared time with each other.

"This is courtesy of the man over there," she gestured to a young man at the corner of the bar. It was one of Sean's team players. She placed the taller glass in front of Sean. "It's four ounces so you might want to take it s-l-o-w-e-r…" Her words dragged off. It was gone! "Well, I guess we won't worry about that. This is for you. It's only two ounces." She smiled. "I'll bring you a diet Pepsi in a moment. Would you like a piece of lemon on the edge?"

Zak smiled, "After these shots, on second thought, please bring two waters for the both of us. No lemon, please."

When she walked away, Zak encouraged Sean to position himself behind the far side of the table. He also persuaded Sean to lower his stool. If he did this, he could innocently look at Sean's groin. He knew Sean's penis was swelling. A lower stool would show more. He watched Sean reached into his pants so his groin was free. The table was higher and had a poster hanging on the front of it. This would hide everything happening behind the table. Zak lusted.

Tonight, Zak and Sean were the only two people in the area. Zak convinced Sean in this area so they had more privacy. Sean was horny, he needed to bust. He did not have sex for a while. When Zak said this, he had no problems agreeing to it because his uncontrollable erections were occurring more often. He now had a wet spot on his pants.

In the process, Zak took two hits of ecstasy and offered Sean one. As his two hits kicked-in, Zak became fixated on where they sat. No one could see their laps. As Sean's hit kicked-in, he became fixated on the bar area and waved to his basketball friends. When he did this, Zak put some Viagra into Sean's water. He knew Sean had a long penis and it would swell.

As Zak sat, he kept innocently looking at Sean and his groin. Sean watched the bar area. He would every now and then stroke his groin. When Sean adjusted his stool, this caused his penis to show more in his pants. Zak could see his penis was out of his cup and getting harder. He loved it.

This was Zak's deceitful side: get a brother high and horny, then play with his swipe. Touch his body to watch him get a full boner. He knew this would turn on Sean. One would have never guessed this from the way he acted, but he did it. As he watched Sean's swipe in his pants. He felt his own penis grow so he hid it.

They sat there smiling and making some small talk. Zak pretended to watched the bar with Sean as they drank, but he kept watching Sean's pants. He saw the bright red color of his athletic cup's strap on his waist. Sean was wearing a small muscle shirt which could not tuck into his pants. He also knew Sean could not hide some of his erections. As he listened to Sean ramble on, he noticed Sean was getting more and more erections. He would get hard then soften. Then, get hard again. Sean naturally pulled on the side of his pants to allow his swipe to move into his leg area.

As Sean got high, his thug side started to show. His talk changed somewhat. Sean got more friendly. However, he was more aggressive. Zak knew he would not hurt him. However, he knew Sean's sexual tension was taking over. He watched Sean constantly rub his hand on his penis and play with his testicles. He felt happy that he had Sean where he wanted him. To sit there and inconspicuously look at his penis harden and soften multiple times turned him on, too.

Zak remembered a time when Sean walked into the locker room after a shower. He had a half hard swipe. He could not believe that he merely held a towel loosely in front of it. Zak of course could not help but look.

What Zak did not know that in Sean's brain, a man's swipe sometimes would swell. He would start to feel that carnal desire to mate. For Sean, it was no big deal. Sometimes he would jag himself multiple times. He would pleasure his body for hours until he could not ejaculate anymore.

* * *

In the bar, it was somewhat like the locker room. Sean started to focus more on Zak. He was feeling his sexual tension. He bumped his shoulder into Zak's, laughed, and touched his swipe. This made his brain tingle: *It sent surges of pleasure throughout his body!* He kept smiling and laughing. He occasionally bumped Zak or pulled on his swipe while they made small talk. Other times, he would sit there playing with himself by grabbing and stroking his meat. He was having pleasure surges. The sports cup was getting to be too much. It was riding on one side of his groin.

Zak was infatuated how Sean could acted so natural about having erections. Sean was so primitive. He looked at him like the tall black beast that wanted sex. He watch him look across the bar and stoke his penis for a minute or two. He sometimes stood, waved to his friends, and worked his fingertips under his penis head while rubbing his thumb across the top. Zak thought he was masturbating in his pants.

* * *

Zak loved it. Zak again thought about the day when they dried off together by their lockers in the workout gym. Sean got a full erection. He had thirteen inches of swipe. Sean stroked it. As they talked, his swipe reduced. Yet, as they got dressed, Zak noted Sean kept pulling on it. Zak swore when Sean stood he had precum dripping off his foreskin.

Zak wanted that long swipe. He was a bit of a size queen. In the locker room, he watched Sean stand in front of him. Zak noted Sean did not care if someone looked at his body; it did not seem to matter.

When Sean sat on the bench to slide up his blue-colored sports cup, Zak could see it standing in the air hanging above his upper leg. His precum started to flow. He watched Sean stroke it again and run the towel across his leg and swipe to wipe his juices off. He stood to get most of it into his cup.

Zak tried to hide an erection. He thought about years ago going to his bedroom to change clothes. His mother would not allow him to touch his frontage in public. He want to masturbate himself right there. Yet, Zak's tighty-whities would help hold him safe. He was G-Q. As a black man, he could not bring himself to show his erection like Sean did.

* * *

In the bar, Zak's thoughts were interrupted by Sean standing off the stool for a moment. He observed him pull and stroke his swipe through his pants. Sean was getting uncomfortable with his harden swipe held by his cup. When he climbed out of the seat, his khakis slid up. Zak could see his meat push out. While standing, Sean pulled his pant legs downward. Once he sat, his khakis slid up again. His swipe was showing more! Zak could tell Sean was obvious to all the actions he displayed. He wanted to see it so bad.

Zak pretended to watched the bar, but his mind focused on Sean's sensation. He watched Sean start moving his leg in and out. Zak was getting more horny watching Sean's penis print on his pants. Zak could tell his banana wanted out to play. Zak so badly wanted to reach over to touch it.

Sean said, "I got to go the bathroom and take off this cup. My swipe is staying hard. I am trying not to look a horny brother, but now I just can't stop it." He laughed. "Sorry, more information than you want to know."

Zak wanted to see something. He wanted to watch him remove his cup. He knew Sean would sometimes do some wild stuff in public if he could get away with it. "Do it right here really quick. The bathroom looks busy right now. If you need to, you know, you can masturbate really fast. Do you need to masturbate? No one will see, stand in front of the table. I'll watch out over the bar." Zak wanted to see his long swipe bounce around.

"You sure?" Sean asked, smiling. "This is crazy. I am about to get naked in public!" He watched Zak nod. Sean loosened his desert boots to slipped them off. He watched the bar area for a moment, then unhooked his belt to get ready. "You watching? Don't let anyone walk up on me. I will be naked," he paused, laughing, "with a half hard swipe."

"Yes. Do it really quick! If someone comes near, I will get up to greet them. Feel good, Sean. If you need help, just ask. I will masturbate you." Zak watched Sean drop his pants. Before Sean could let his pants go, Zak grabbed his cup to help slide it down. "We got to hurry…" When he saw Sean's penis, he stopped talking. He watched Sean's swipe bounced out and wiggle around. The trunk was set free. He could see precum. "You need to cum?"

"You are watching?" Sean replied. "Zak?"

"Yes." Zak watched Sean start to put his pants on again. Zak loved how his groin was all shaven except a little patch of hair above his shaft.

"Zak, I'm trying to change. Stop looking at me. It will only keep it hard longer." Sean stroked himself. He suddenly heard some people talking while walking out of the bathroom area. He sat quickly.

Zak noticed Sean forgot to zip his zipper. Zak was now in heaven! His brain was tingling from the visual pleasures. He saw Sean's trunk staying fully hard. "You need to cum?"

Zak felt compelled to adjust his clothes to be sure they were perfect; yet, innocently, he touched his own penis. He could see Sean was not watching. Zak had a full erection.

He lusted for Sean's swipe while he rubbed it! It was so long and hard.

* * *

Eventually, Sean pulled the bar stool closer to Zak and sat on the edge of it. "It feels better to have my cup off." Now it slid down the side of his pant leg. Being with another gay man, Sean felt comfortable; someone like him. He thought about what Zak said about jagging off. His thug side ran with it. After moments of thinking about it, he literally put his hand into his open fly. He pulled his shaft out of his pants to stroke himself. "O-o-p-s, I forgot to zip this!" He laughed. It felt so good to touch it. He did not even bother to put his swipe back in his pants. "I am sticking out." He trailed, high. "I need sex. You cool if I jerk myself? You said I need to jerk off."

Zak took a chance. "Lift yourself off the stool so I can open your pants more." He took Sean's belt out of the front two loops of his pants, then loosely re-buckled it. Zak unclipped Sean's pants to loosen them. While he did this, he made sure he fumbled around so he could touch his penis. Once done, he touched Sean's hand on the table. "How you doing over there?"

With the other, he put a finger on Sean's penis tip.

"Wow, Zak, I really felt that. It's like my body came alive." Sean looked at his hand. The gentle touch by someone else put Sean's brain traveling in a new direction. "Everything I touch is great. I can even feel a little bit of the air moving in here." He had a half grin stuck on his face. "Even my clothes when I move, they make me feel great!"

Sean casually scratched his nuts. "Keep touching my swipe. Touch me more."

Zak noticed when he did this to Sean, his swipe would stick up more. Sometimes it bounced out of his hand. He saw he had juices flowing. He giggle as he touched it, "Sean, your penis is really swollen and feels so warm in my hand. I knew you needed sex." He wanted to treat Sean. Zak started to stroke it. "Slide the stool closer to me. It feels good, doesn't it?" He slowly teased Sean by working his foreskin back and forth over his penis head.

"Yeah, that feels so good. I need to cream," Sean's brain was heading to its pleasure zone. He was high and horny. "The way your fingertips are massaging my swipe is making me tingle." Sean rambled on some more at how great it felt. "It sometimes happens to me, I get erections. Damn, I don't have my sports cup on. I took it off?" Sean put his hand on his swipe, he pushed Zak's hand off, he wanted to rub it. He felt Zak push it away so he could not rub it. "Fuck, now I got to lean on the table so people don't think I am a pervert." He laughed, again. "You're making the tip all creamy."

"Let me work your skin back and forth more." Zak pulled his hood all the way back.

Sean looked around the bar again, "Zak, what are you doing?"

Zak played with his foreskin. He made it slide up and down to collect his juices on the end of his swipe. When he did this, it made it slide so easy. Zak replied, "I need to get your skin back as far as I can so I can stroke your head." Zak started to play with Sean's penis head.

Sean watched the crowd, waved to a few basketball friends, "good idea". Sean looked down at himself, he pushed Zak's hand off to rub his swipe a few times, "It will go down eventually." He laughed, "Just keep working it. You can get a cum shot." He trailed in laughter. "I'm commando right now…"

Zak reached over, pushing his big swipe downward.

Sean looked down, "Oh that felt great. What are you doing now?"

"Just playing. I can do something else!" Zak grinned. He moved his own pants around to get them perfect, this allowed him to rubbed across his own erection. He had it pushed between his leg. When he wiggled his own legs, he could feel the pressure on it. Now, he worked it upward so it was looser and he could rub on his own head.

"What? What you got in mind?"

"Lean a little forward and don't play with yourself so much," Zak giggled again. He was getting other ideas in his mind about what to do.

Sean complied, he looked over the crowd. "I'm down!" When Sean put his hands back on the table, he leaned on his elbows. It felt so good. He then looked at Zak's meat sticking upward in his pants. "I see your thick swipe, I wish I could taste it. I love how fat it is."

"You like Master Zak's penis?" Zak smiled.

"Yeah, I want to feel it in my mouth," Sean moaned. He felt Zak hands touching his swipe, then his back side. Every now and then, Zak would push his hand into his nuts.

Zak then ran one of his hands up Sean's shirt feeling his erect nipples. "My cum doggie will be able to lick and suck it in due time."

"O-o-h, that feels so carnal right now." Sean started wiggling his legs back and forth to feel the sensation. "I got to stand," Sean stood upward. "Touch my swipe more. Get me off!"

Zak looked at Sean with his penis under the table, "Stand there for a little bit, my little doggy," he watched Sean smile.

"Yeah, just tell me if someone walks up!" He trailed off in gentle laughter.

Zak rubbed his fingertips on Sean's swipe hair and the top of his shaft. "I like how you shave your penis hair! It looks sexy." He was taking his time loving every minute of it. "I think my little doggie needs a masturbation session!"

"Damn, Zak, I'm horny and you doing me like this? In public?" Sean was loving it, too. "Jag that fucker off for me, get me off faster! I need to cream."

Zak took his hand off to have a drink. "Not too fast." He took his thumb and two fingers to lightly massage Sean head and foreskin area. Every two or three gentle touches, he would run a fingertips on his tight nut sack. Zak lusted as he watched his full erection. Sometimes it would bounce around on its own. Sometimes it pumped juice. "I need to play with this some more."

Sean laughed, high. "I have dropped all my boundaries to see this glimpse of what I should be." He felt Zak's touches looking down now and then to watch. "We are sexual beings that necd to release. Do you agree? We're here to cum?" Precum ran from his swipe. "I feel so carnal, Zak, keep doing it! Here in public makes me feel even more horny. Pull on my tight nuts so I can feel it."

"My little cum doggy's penis head is all wet and pocking out of its skin!" Zak look at Sean's long, thick shaft. He played with his skin. "Let me rub it some more! You need a good masturbation job. I like doing that to you. I will get your sperm out. Your testicles are swollen, too."

Sean brought his hand down to rub on Zak's swipe. "I feel your fat meat." Then he grabbed the bottom of his own shaft to stroke it and hit his nuts.

Each time he grabbed himself, Zak would push his hand away, "stop that, my little cum doggy. You're always playing with yourself. You masturbate too much!"

It turned Sean on even more, "yes…s-o-r-r-y." But, he did it again. "You're a freaky fucker, Zak!" His hard dick stood out, rock hard at thirteen. Precum was dripping faster.

Zak felt Sean's muscles under his nuts start to contract. "You know I work in the clinical building, I know about a man's sexual arousal."

"I know…"

"You know, Master Zak," he replied. "Now say it!"

"I know, Master Zak. I need my swipe to be jagged off by someone else to get out all my cream."

"That's better, my cum doggie!" Zak watched his penis dripped a little sperm out. If Sean's juices started to flow, Zak would purposely let his penis go. This would cause Sean to drip out more. "I have to masturbate you good! My cum doggy is horny tonight!" He started playing with him more watching his penis head. "Let me squeezed these nuts because my cum doggie will shoot more sperm!" He had both hands on Sean.

"I'm dripping cum," Sean ran his fingers on his swipe head feeling the stickiness. He stuck his finger into Zak's

26

mouth, "That's for you." He separated his leg apart a little further. "Don't stop, Zak!"

Zak's hand started to move up and down faster, he grabbed a napkin to clean Sean's swipe head of fluids. He watched Sean move around as he did it. He was lusting for it. Sean's head was pulsating in his hand. He let it go, "Not yet my cum doggy! Not yet!" He watched more sperm ooze out of his little slit on his penis head.

"Come on, Master Zak, jag me, please," Sean look forward at the crowd, "please, please, please."

"In due time." Zak suddenly noticed Sean had a little greater cum surge.

"I see Master Zak likes to play with it." Sean reach around Zak to rub a finger on his booty. "I want to help you!" He smiled.

"Good, my little cum doggy. I need to feel good, too!" Zak giggled. Zak rubbed as fast as he could. He watched Sean back up from the table just enough to look down to watch. Zak watched Sean stare at his one hand pumping his swipe and the other pulling on his nuts. He watched Sean bend his knees and push his groin out more.

"O-o-h, that feels so good! Make me cum, Master Zak! Please, please, please."

Zak started rubbing his own penis while Sean put both hand on the table. Zak smiled, "how's my little doggy doing. Is his mind racing with cumming thoughts?" He kept whispering dirty comments that he knew Sean liked to hear. "You want to cum, little doggy?"

"Yes, Master Zak," Sean moaned in pleasure. "Make me cum; hard!"

"I will. You are being a good cum doggy!" He felt Sean's outer rim of his penis head stretched as far as it could go, "is my little doggy gonna cum?" He pulled harder on his nuts. Suddenly, Sean couldn't control himself. He got quieter and started breathing heavier.

"Being that you are a good cum doggie today, I'm going to milk you from the backside." Zak felt his hand get wetter and creamed up around Sean's head, his dick starting going up and down. Sean laid his chest on the table. Zak grabbed his meat from the backside with three fingers to jerk his head as fast as he could. "My cum doggy gonna shoot?" Zak pulled on his nuts stretching them upward.

"O-o-o-h, f-u-c-k…" Sean was moaning heavily. "Keep pulling my nuts. Kept doing it!"

Zak put his full hand around his swipe pounding it up and down. He pulled Sean's nuts up more. He squeezed them hard. He watched Sean lay his arms across the table. Now Zak could pound his swipe with ease. Zak's fingers easily slipped up and down. Once he felt Sean start to cum, he let his nuts go to hold the napkin under his draining penis. Zak felt his rhythmic muscle contractions. Sean released into the napkin.

Zak watched Sean at first spray out cum. It hit the napkin hard. There were three tight contractions, then two more sprays. He could see the area behind his nut pulsate. Then it flowed more steadily. Sean was like a river now. As it flowed, he watched a great deal more ooze out. Once Zak stopped, he wiped the tip with another napkin. He noticed every time he wiped, Sean grabbed the table harder.

"Zak, be easy, it is sensitive right now," Sean said.

"My little cum doggy gonna disobey?" He gently pulled on his nuts.

"O-o-o-h. N-o," Sean moaned, "I'll be your cum doggy!" Sean's body jerked again, "wipe it off," he paused again, "Master Zak…"

As Zak kept wiping, he loved watching Sean struggle. "Come on, my little doggy, I have to get it clean." He watched Sean try to pull away, but he wouldn't release his testicles until he was all done. "Proper hygiene, Sean." As Zak finished, he busted himself. He sprayed his cum on Sean's upper leg.

* * *

When they were done, Sean slipped on his athletic cup and pants. Zak tuck his swipe away into his briefs, then proceeded to get his perfect dressed code. Sean was still horny, he liked playing with Master Zak! He liked their masturbation secession. They had a great night.

Sean was hoping their relationship would go further.

* * *

The lights were flashing: blue, red, white, and yellow. The officer had Sean planted on the hood of his car. Sean knew something was wrong! His enjoyable evening just had to end this way. The officers told him to spread his legs further apart, he kept rubbing his nightstick between his legs.

"I didn't do anything," Sean firmly stated. Sean felt the officer still do it so he clenched his fists.

"Boy, you gonna give me problems?"

"No sir!"

At that point, Sean felt a sudden excruciating pain in his groin. The officer pulled the handle of the stick up as hard as he could. Sean fell on the hood of his car. Then, he felt the officer lift his T-shirt and taser him. He fell on the black top pissing his pants. The officer knelt down putting a knee into his gut. "The taser will work better on your wet spot."

Sean felt another, longer zap to his groin.

"Fuck," he yelled. As the voltage flowed throughout his body, he could not even talk.

* * *

Once in the back of the squad car Sean sat quietly. When the officers placed him in the car, he rammed his mouth into the roof top. If the officer asked him any questions, he only replied, 'yes sir' or 'no sir'. He was afraid the officer might hurt him some more. He could taste the blood on his lip.

* * *

This evening was so pleasurable yet, the officer immediately took it all away. His thug side took over his thoughts. The fun time he had with Zak was now gone, he had a heart filled with hatred.

2. Supper with Sis

My women, Kay, knew Sean was hanging a little with her younger brother. Sean and Kal were not seeing anyone else on a steady basis so she decided we all should have a meal together. At this time, our quiet lives were moving along together.

* * *

Within moments, Kal stepped through the door. "Thanks for inviting me over, Sis, sorry I'm late."

"We started without you. Grab a plate," Kay replied. "I was just telling Sean you might be a little late."

"Kay, do you want to pull the table away from the wall for a place where Kal can sit? It will give us more room," I asked unsuspectingly. The woman kicked me in the shin! *Glad she only had on socks!*

"If we do that, I have to push it back again, so I can slide it down to place it in front of the door. I just don't feel like doing all that tonight. If it's okay with Sean, Kal can sit next to him. There is plenty of room." Kay had this big old heavy table in her kitchen. It was about four feet by eight feet. At night, she moved it in front of her apartment door for protection. I wanted her to move further out of Chicagoland, yet she had her day job in this area so she never would move.

* * *

This was prior to Sean being stopped by the police officer. Kay liked family time together and wanted us all over for dinner. We will get to the police part soon. Needless to say, when it did occur I was not a happy camper. She wanted her brother: Kal; and Sean to be able to have a quiet night together, too. She was up to something with Sean and Kal, I just did not know what.

* * *

I sat directly across from Sean and Kal. Kay was sitting on the corner next to me. We were so far apart from them, she would sometimes actually get up to pass the food down.

"I don't care," Sean replied. "I understand the ghetto, Mama Kay. Home security is important! We all have to be safe."

"So, how are you doing, player?" Kal asked, as he sat down next to him. "I haven't seen you for a minute. Kay said you went to county."

"I'm good. Things have been cool, lately."

Kay and Kal talked with each other, then Kal and Sean talked. So, Kay and I talked. We were having a good time. I kicked her lightly! I figured out what she was doing.

Kal looked around the table for the salt and pepper. He ate with his right hand careful not to have his left hand on the table. Now that he was at his sister's place, he was on his best behavior. He had such good manners.

"Oh, Kal," Kay broke off our conversation for a moment, "I told Sean you were wondering how he was doing. I mentioned you were looking forward to seeing him again."

"Yeah, I was player. When you were here last time, I had fun. You been cool? How did county go?"

"Yeah. I'm good. What can I say about county? County is county! I had fun last time, too." Sean notice Kal wasn't so strong in his thug role. This was the third time he was around him. The first time he acted like a little pit bull ready to bite. When they were out, only alone did he noticed Kal dropped it. If other men came around, he started the thug routine. This time he dropped the role completely. He was being gentle and polite. "I see you eased up on the street thug routine. You had me fooled."

"This is Chicagoland! Motherfuckers will take advantage!" Kal replied, harshly. He then smiled, dropping his attitude, "just saying. I'm different than what you think. I have a cool side."

"So, Kay, how is work?" I asked. I noticed Kay slide her seat down closer to mine. Probably wanted to kick me again.

As Kay and I talked, Kal got Sean's attention. "So, player, how's your basketball game doing?"

"Well," Sean started. He put his left hand in his lap to rub his groin, with his right he forked some food. "It is still cold. Play almost every day. Yours?"

"Great." Kal grabbed Sean's hand on his lap to squeeze it. "Glad to hear, brotha." Sean's attention immediately went to his hand being squeezed. He noticed as they continued to talk, Kal kept touching his arm. Finally, Kal laid his hand on his leg.

Sean looked at me and Kay. He noticed we could not see anything Kal was doing. He now felt Kal's hand gently rubbing the inside of his upper leg area. "Yeah, I am seeing a different Kal!" He whispered.

"You're a good b-ball player," Kal peeped Sean's lap seeing his dick making a print on his pants. "Told you I was different. Kay said something to me about you. On the court, your game looked good and so did you."

They both were whispering comments.

Sean took a scoop of fried cabbage then coughed, "A-h-e-m; sorry, too big of a scoop!" He felt Kal's wrist move over his swipe head.

"You okay, player?" Kal asked. He then ran his hand across Sean's pipe. Kal stared at him with a concerned look, "to big of a bite? Kay's fried cabbage is good."

"Sean, you okay?" Mama Kay spoke.

Kay and I both looked down to the far end of the table.

"Yeah. Let me use the bathroom to blow my nose," Sean said. He grabbed his hoodie while staring at Kal. "I think some food went up there. I'll be back in a moment." Sean was careful to stand so Unck and Mama Kay could not see the lump by his zipper. He had his sports cup on but sometimes it was not enough. The hoodie helped.

When Sean stood, Kal innocently stared at his swipe. It naturally pushed on his zipper. It looked like a large banana. Sean's blue elastic strap of his athletic cup showed a little above the top of his pants. Kal figured he had everything all snugly tucked away. "I'll show you were it is," Kal commented. "It's down the hallway."

When Kal led Sean to the bathroom, he naturally touched Sean's lower back. "You sure are big. How tall are you?"

Sean felt a few of his fingers play with the back of the strap on his cup. "I see you are different." When Sean stood in the bathroom, he kept talking. Once he blew his nose, he faced Kal fully to open his pants. "I'm about six foot six." He began to readjust the cup he was wearing. "I'm big everywhere," Sean smiled, reaching his hand into his sports cup to stroke and adjust himself. "You like my blue sports cup? It's designer like undies." He stood in front of Kal watching him look at his swipe. He rubbed his fingers over it.

It went a little faster than Kal expected. It was a sensuous moment to watch him run his fingers around the cup and pull it down a bit to fit his swipe better. "Yes! It's sexy. I see you have two cuts in your muscles going to your swipe, you stay in shape," Kal replied. "I think I should get back to the table before Sis and your uncle start wondering where we are at."

"You running off already? Did I scare you?"

When Sean was done using the bathroom, he quickly made a decision to see how far Kal would go with him. He slipped off his sports cup to go commando. He naturally gave his swipe some pulls wondering what Kal looked like naked. He wondered if he really liked him.

"Hope we didn't scare big-bird and Kal away," I chuckled. This time I moved my leg so Kay couldn't kick it. "Maybe it was your cooking," I laughed.

"Whitey…"

As Kal made it back to sit down, we both got quiet.

When Sean came back, he noticed Kay and I were chattering away, again. Sean took a moment, quietly murmuring to Kal, "Want to keep my pants up so I don't get in trouble. No sagging in Mama Kay's house!" He knew Kay had that thing about proper dress code!

Kal smiled, looking at him. "She has rules." Kal looked at Sean's beautiful towering body.

He knew he had an athletic build. It was apparent by his dress. His waist was not more than twenty-eight to thirty inches. "A brother got to be careful; I gotcha! No sense starting an argument. I'm like Kay, no drama." He could see Sean's long beautiful swipe hanging delightfully behind his zipper. Once out of the sports cup, it pressed harder on his pants giving a nice long print. Due to the length of his swipe, it hung just below the end of the zipper showing a tip. He notice Sean carried his hoodie so neither Kay nor I could see.

Sean saw him looking at his swipe so he took his fingers to slightly cup the tip. He flicked it upward a few times. He jacked his slacks to loosen the right side of his pant leg. Then, he grabbed the end of the zipper to shake his meat. He whispered, "if I bring my pants up, I have to adjust myself down there when I sit. If I don't, it will get uncomfortable."

"No worries; don't want to be uncomfortable," Kal replied, smiling. He watched every minute of it. "Got to look good in my Sis's house. You look very good. I like your mohawk. The tint of red fits you well. Your short mustache and goatee looks 'GQ'; player like."

Sean sat for a second. "Thanks. You look good, too. I think I have to do it again; adjust myself," he whispered. He pulled on his pant leg to loosen it, then worked his swipe up so it could run down his leg. "Sorry, I know it shows more but it isn't so tight." It looked like a log laying there on his inner pant leg. "That's better."

"I see you decided to remove your cup," Kal noted. "That must be tight. You have quite the log down there!"

"Yeah, I was just getting uncomfortable." Sean grabbed his meat pulling it to feel the pleasure of the strokes. He pushed the right side of his hoodie behind him between the back of the chair. "Got to get straight. You know, comfortable with someone cool. Sometimes, I get a hard swipe going commando; everything moving and rubbing around."

"Nothing taken. You look good." Kal occasionally look at Sean's lap, being commando he could see his full swipe print on the leg of his khakis. He watched Sean as they talked. Sean kept touching the head of his swipe and gripping its shaft. "Ain't it a little cold for those thin khakis?" He started again to rub on Sean's leg. He pinched the material. "Things will get cold."

"That's why I kept my hoodie on." Sean moved his right leg back and forth, every now and then he bumped Kal's knee, "O-o-p-s, sorry."

"You a player, it happens," Kal replied, rubbing Sean's leg. "Your size takes up a lot of space. I am only five foot nine. I get it. You're so big if you move, you bump someone not meaning to. I liked seeing your 6-pack stomach while playing ball."

Sean shifted his chair closer to Kal watching Kay and I gab and watch a video on her phone. "I keep hitting this table leg on my side." When he did this, it forced Kal's hand to slide down his inner leg on his meat. "Oh, sorry. Excuse me." Sean could feel the charge shooting from his groin, up his back and to his brain.

"No harm, not like it is the first swipe I touched," Kal whispered, smiling. He placed his hand back on Sean's leg noticing his meat was starting to lengthen and climb up his pant leg. "I like swipe!" He smiled.

He felt Sean's leg move back and forth a few times. His meat was rubbing against the material.

"Food is good. Your sister cooks well."

"Yes, she does." Kal was trying to determine the length of it. When he felt it, it reminded him of an elephant trunk. So, he slid his hand back on it to work the loose fabric around it. Kal watched Sean widen out his legs. When Sean did this, he could feel more of its length.

"How is everything going down there, Unck?" Sean asked Kay and I. "What you watching on Mama Kay's phone?"

"What?" I watched Kay pause the video.

"What you watching?"

"Oh. These funny driving videos."

"Must be good; enjoy." Sean watched Mama Kay start the video again.

"They must like those," Sean commented to Kal. "Glad it's loud!" Sean had to readjust himself again. He grabbed the top of Kal's hand lifting on his swipe. It was pointing upward now. He had a wet spot on his pant leg. He brought his legs together for a second, then with both their hands he worked his shaft up toward the pocket area of his pants.

Kal smiled, "getting more comfortable, I see." Kal wiggled his fingers on it while Sean held his hand. "Maybe one day I can see it; see your full body?"

"Yeah," he said softly. Sean was focusing on his sensation. He maneuvered his shaft so it laid on the top of his leg. He slid down in the set so he wasn't straighter. He felt Kal's palm and fingers caressing the top of it. "I'm glad to be here with you, Kal. I like no drama! Like I said, sometimes I get erections being around someone cool."

"Me too. I get them, too. I'm glad to see you, again," Kal replied, sitting back a little, too. "Two players just chilling over supper."

Kay's phone shut off. Kal calmly slid his hand back to his lap. The room was quieter now.

"Excuse me, you two," Kay said, smiling, "We're going into the living room for wine, do you want to join us?" Kay nor I knew what was really occurring under the table.

"No, I got to finish this meal," Kal replied. He casually reached for some water with his left hand.

"I'm not done yet, either," Sean said. "This fried cabbage is the bomb, Mama Kay. Plus, I want to catch up with Kal. That cool, Unck?"

"Sure. Kay, you cool?"

"Yeah, if you two want to catch up. If you want, you can join us later." Kay smiled at her brother, "just say something if you join us."

With us gone, Kal whispered in Sean's ear, "they're rubbing them noses, we should not go in there for a while." When he leaned toward Sean's ear, he naturally rested his hand back on his swipe print. Kal started to massage Sean even harder. He watched him move his chair back and side further down. "I like the feel of your meat."

"Move your chair back, too." Sean played with his swipe to make it as visible as possible.

"Feels good, don't it? I'm enjoying it." Kal started stroking it again. Kal's voice became very sensuous. "You are a big dick brother. I see you got some inches. It lays like a log across your leg."

"I know," Sean smiled. "If you keep touching it, I will want more." He put his arm around Kal and move his chair against his. "I like booty. I like to give chocolate dick downs."

Kal looked at him, "I like swipe. I want to suck on it! To see how it tastes!" As he said that, he noticed Sean lengthened fully. He kissed Sean and massaged him harder.

"O-o-o-h," Sean moaned quietly.

"Let me get it off really quick," Kal rubbed his khakis harder and faster. He watched Sean get quiet, his stomach moved then suddenly he felt his swipe in his pants start to pulsate up and down. Kal quickly unzipped his pants. "I'm…I'm gonna bust in my pants." Sean stopped everything to grabbed the table. His pleasure flows were coming faster and faster. He felt a bare hand grab his swipe.

"How's that working?" Kal said, softly. Sean's meat was ejaculating sperm as he pulled it out. Kal put his other hand in front of it, "let me see your cum shot!" He felt his penis lift up with each squirt of juice. "Feels good don't it!" He teased. He looked at Sean head totally exposed so he kept working his fingers on it.

Sean spread out his legs, looking down at Kal's hands. He instinctively thrust his loins, "o-o-h, fuck." More came out, then he relaxed.

"Here, let me wipe it off." Kal grab a table towel to wipe it. He watched his head start to retract into its foreskin. "That is a lot of cum!"

Sean was worried, "What about your Sis and Unck? What if they come out here? You got me busting. Unck will kill me! Kay will be on you, too!"

Kal replied, "You saw them rubbing noses, they won't come out here. You hear the shower running, they're both in there." Kal smiled, "I liked what I saw! Can I get more?"

"Okay," Sean stood. "You want some more of my jism?"

Kal stared at Sean's length. His swipe was laying outside his pants. Kal began to naturally pucker his lips. He didn't even realize he was doing it. "Let me taste it," he whispered. His tongue wet his lips. "Can I taste it?"

"Okay," he slipped out of his shoes and dropped pants. When he moved his swipe closer to Kal's lips, he watched him again naturally lick them. "I see you want to suck something!"

"I sure do."

"Show me how good you are at sucking out jism." Sean instinctively massaged his nuts anticipating Kal's lips on his swipe.

Kal lengthen his neck and started to suck on Sean's swipe head. Eventually, he felt Sean begin to again harden. His penis lengthened out in his mouth. Kal quickly rubbed his tongue on the bottom of his swipe head, them swallowed more of his shaft. It was so long he couldn't get it all in.

When he backed off for a moment, he asked, "How long is this thing? A foot!" He took a breath. He started sucking again.

"You're a freak!" Sean chuckled. "It hangs at thirteen when I'm cumming! It is still going to grow." He grabbed one of Kal's hands placing it on his nut sack, "pull hard on my tight nuts, I love that shit! Wrap your thumb and finger around them to force them outward."

Kal focused on his two beautiful nuts under his shaft. They were like two golf balls hanging in his tight scrotum. He locked his hand around them tightening his thumb and forefinger. He could barely stretch them.

"Y-e-a-h," Sean moaned, taking one leg out of pants so he could spread them apart, "work them nuts and swipe."

As Kal gave him a blowjizzle, he lusted at his beautiful muscular body towering over him. "Hold up for a second, player," he pulled down his own pants. Kal had seven inches of swipe with a reddish head. There was a creamy juice sweeping out of it. Kal was now in his pure pleasure zone: playing with himself and sucking on a dick. "I love getting off with a dick in my mouth!" He pulled himself faster. "It's so big."

"I see…" Sean paused to moan. "You got the swipe?"

Kal could feel Sean's shaved nut sack which made his thoughts run wild. "I got the dick. You got this ass?" Kal pulled on Sean's nuts and sucked harder. He thought about that sensuous picture of seeing Sean in his khakis going commando. Now, he knew why his swipe shaft pressed so hard on the front of them. His large tight nuts forced his shaft to hang over them which pushed it out further from his body.

His tongue licked on the bottom of his head. He pictured Sean rising from the chair with his khakis surrounding his long swipe hanging to one side of his pants. As he swallowed it, he rolled his tongue around it. Kal begin to finger himself as he lusted at the thought of being penetrated. "I got the dick. You got my ass?"

Sean spread his legs further apart by placing one foot on a chair. Out of sexual instinct, he reached down grabbing Kal hand on his nuts making him squeeze and pull harder. He stared at Kal sucking on him. "O-o-h," he quietly moaned, "eat that sh-zit! A-w-w-w-w-w." He forced Kal's hand to reached behind his nut sack and take his fingers to pinch that area, too. "I'm a freak, I want to feel it. I got that ass if you can handle this dick!"

Kal sucked away looking up at him. His beautiful brown eyes stared at his reaction on his face. He quickly pulled off his T-shirt, "I need more of your swipe. I'm gonna to jag you to get a facial of cum!" Kal started to pull on himself faster and faster! He consumed as much of his shaft as he could.

When Sean heard what Kal said, it was over! "I'm gonna bust." Sean put a hand on Kal's head. He felt Kal pull off, but Sean held him on. He was climaxing again, "o-o-o-o-o-h, I'm nuttin," he groaned, "suck it, baby!"

Kal quickly, but gently stroked his swipe. This slowed Sean's climax. "Give me that facial."

"A-w-w." Sean's mind took over, he lost all train of thought. Sean jerked around uncontrollably. He could feel his sperm flowing up his pipe. "Pull on it, Kal!" The gentle touch he felt on his head and shaft made him climax harder with greater uncontrollable contractions.

His body released more testosterone and thrust more blood into his swipe. Sean started pulling on his own nuts.

Kal could feel the first cum drops hit his face. Sean's muscles in his loins rhythmically thrust blood into his meat. "Cum on me, baby." He watched Sean staring at the while unable to do anything, but cum.

At a few squirts, Sean managed to move. He grabbed Kal's hair and bent his neck back. Everything focused on as his organism as it ran uncontrollably through his body. He grabbed his pulsating pipe to jerk himself harder. "Here, Bitch, you want some cum!"

"Yes, please; y-e-s," Kal stared at Sean face when he grabbed his hair, "m-o-r-e b-a-b-y!" He stuck his tongue out. All those cum drops on his face made him spray, too!

When it was over, Sean put the end of his poll into Kal mouth, "clean that shit off". Sean stood over Kal as their bodies began to return to normal. Sean's erection dropped to eleven, then ten inches. He grabbed Kal's hair, "you like it rough? You cool with this so far?"

Kal slid his clothes on. As he did, he watched Sean's foreskin naturally side half over his swipe head. His swipe was still hanging at nine long inches. Sean grabbed his athletic cup to slide it on. "I like it baby. I want to feel it in me!" Kal smiled. "We ain't done yet, I got an idea."

"Good," Sean whispered, "cause I want a shot of your booty!" Sean buckled his belt. Then, Sean rubbed Kal's print on his jeans, "you gonna have to get off with me in you. Think you can take it?"

Kal smiled ear to ear, again, "yeah!"

44

Suddenly, they both heard Mama Kay's voice from the back. They scrambled for chairs to sit kitty-corner at the table. "Is it okay if I come out?"

"Yeah, Sis, we just talking."

"How you two doing out here? Whitey and I are going to bed." She stood filling the wine glasses, again.

"Sean and I are going to chill on the porch, watch the sky, and have a few beers," Kal replied. "Is that cool?"

"Okay; well, you two have fun together," she smiled. "Don't forget when you come in to side the table in front of the door. See you in the morning."

"You want to go on the porch, it is nice outside," Kal smiled. "My Sis has a grill that acts like a heater and some warmers. We can close the blinds. It's got screening so the bugs won't get us."

"Okay, but I got to run to the bathroom."

"I'll get a couple of 40s out of the refrigerator."

* * *

I heard the back door close. "Kay, did they go out?" I asked, lying on the bed.

"Only to the porch, they are going to have a couple of beers."

"Hum; wonder what else they might be doing?" I smiled at her.

"Now, Whitey; that is not our business. Help me with my bra strap."

I sat up, "O-h, you know I am good with that!" I chuckled, grinning.

"And, you wonder where Sean gets it from!" Kay switched subjects, "how has Sean been adjusting with his family situation?" She was concerned. "I know it has been awhile. What do you think?"

"We sometimes talk. You know his mother hurt him, but he is improving. He is almost thirty, I hope he clicks one day. He does not challenge me like he use too." I stared at her face next to me. She had those beautiful brown eyes.

"How about his father? You know, his death?"

"He blames his mother for that. I doubt he will ever try to see her again."

"I just hope he stops getting into trouble with the law doing that petty stuff," she noted.

"Me too, baby, me too. When we talk about that, he throws it back in my face reminding me that I have been there, too. Yet, he is more open to listen now." I touched my finger to her nose.

"I see you want to rub noses again," Kay smiled, putting her arm around me.

"Sure do," I gave her a kiss. "Kay, we just have to keep showing him our love. You just keep doing what you do."

"I agree. Now hold me." Kay pushed me back on the bed and climbed on top to embrace me with her love. "Give me that shit, Whitey."

* * *

Kal and Sean were sitting on one of the lawn chairs. When Sean sat, Kal climbed onto his lap. They both removed their shirts. Kal started grinding on his lap with his ass. He lusted about Sean's beautiful cut body, it was

46

perfect. "I love how you have taken care of yourself. I love running my hands over it. I like how you cut you fro into a mohawk. I can tell you like the color red."

"Let me unbutton your pants," Sean said, passionately. He slid his hands slowly around Kal's waist, clutching him as he was being ridden.

"I got a blunt, you want some?" Kal questioned. He felt Sean slid his pants down a little to tenderly run his hands in the sides of his jeans. "I also got some V-i-a-g-r-a," Kal's voice softly lifted. "I need a good fucking." He kissed him.

"Damn," Sean laughed, "you want to fuck all night! I think I can do that: buck wild and fuck wild!"

"I hope so. Can you keep up with me! I love to fuck! I love sex. I want to see you in that blue designer cup!"

Kal got up to turn the grill up higher and partly lower the three blinds in front of them. He lowered the ones to the left and right. The middle one he lowered a third of the way down. They could still see the skyline from the fourth-floor porch. He stood in front of Sean as they both took some pills. His pants still had his print on them. "I need to take off these pants." Kal's dick was already hard from grinding.

Sean got up to take his pants off. He smiled, "You want to see me in my cup? R-I-g-h-t?" His swipe pushed out on his cup. He walked around a little while talking. He lit the blunt. "I need to fuck."

"I really like your blue cup, it looks so sexy on you. Blue is my favorite color. I also like how you trimmed your hairs on your penis." He pulled open the front of Sean's cup to look. "And, those shaved nuts; it feels like baby skin!" He massaged the cup briefly.

"I like your body, too." He lifted Kal's hand to look at him. "You got tight nuts, too. I think you have a little more than seven inches and your cut penis head has a nice rim on it." He played with Kal's nipples. "You lucky you have less body hair than me."

"I got a tight ass. I don't give it up to every dog on the block." Kal smile, "we just to gay brothers, broad nose and bigger lips, living in America!"

As Sean smoked, he kissed Kal. "I cut my body hair because I don't like all that hair. I don't have much anyways. When I be jagging, I love feeling the skin on my nuts!" He forced his tongue into Kal's mouth.

Kal lifted on his pipe in the cup, "we'll point it upward. We don't want it to break. It could be a long night." He chuckled. He did his best to tuck it into the top of the cup. He looked at Sean's big nuts push out on the bottom of it. He rubbed them with his palm and kissed Sean again, "you sure got some big, tight nuts!" Kal started licking Sean's nipples.

"Yeah, that's one reason why I wear the cup. They push my swipe outward, people think I'm horny all the time even when I'm not!" He chuckled, "my mama told me I had the curse so I should dress appropriately." Sean sat back down in the chair. "I like wearing a cup, it holds everything in. You know how when you are walking or moving, your swipe rubs on shit. Sometimes, I get erections feeling it."

Kal stared at him sitting, occasionally looking down at the bulge in his cup. He reached down, "let me feel it some more." Kal noticed Sean swipe filled it and then some. He love how his meat naturally pressed hard against the top of it and his big nuts filled the bottom so beautifully. "I'm getting horny."

Sean laughed, "if I get hard in public, I can't hide it! I go out with dudes, but they complain about its size."

Kal smiled, "or, god gave you a nice blessing. He gave you tight nuts and a long swipe. He gave you a beautiful trunk. Every man wishes for a long swipe. I only got seven inches."

Sean smiled, then he licked on the sides of Kal's swipe. He rolled his tongue and licked on his head. He felt Kal squirm so he held him tighter as he give him a blowjizzle. "I like how the ridge of penis stands out so far. It isn't about the size, it is what it can do, baby." He licked his tongue around it and took it back in. He took a fast moment to talk, "I like your swipe, it tastes good and perfectly fits in my mouth!" Sean straighten his neck to let it slide into his throat.

Kal played with both of his nipples. He saw Sean's swipe pushing harder on his cup. It infatuated him even more! "I need to play with my booty hole."

"I will be playing with it in a minute. You can wait. It's gonna be a long night."

"Okay." Kal grabbed a rubber ring laying on the table next to them. He bent over, pushing Sean back.

Sean lifted himself so he could pull off his cup. He watched Kal stretch it around his swipe and nuts. "That will make you hornier."

"I see you got that freaky side." Sean rub himself as he sucked Kal's swipe some more. He spread his leg further apart so he could rock his nuts on the lawn chair. When he looked up, Kal was staring at him sucking on his dick. He kept staring at him.

"I see you rubbing them tight nuts on the chair. You are a freak, too!" Kal put his foot between Sean's legs for a moment to watch and feel him run his nuts over his sock. "You like to treat your nuts ruff!" He grabbed Sean's hair to pull on it.

Sean came off him, "yeah!" Then, got busy again for about ten minutes. He felt Kal tense up. Kal's pulling on his hair was turning him on. So, he started rubbing Kal's booty with one hand and his belly with the other. He massaged his booty hole with one finger. Occasionally, he would insert the tip of it into him. Then, it was two fingers.

"Fuck that feels great!" Kal's head fell back.

"I like your swipe. I got the dick!" Sean stretched out his neck, swallowing all of Kal again.

Suddenly, Kal's swipe swelled as hard as it could and his nuts pulled tight. Sean felt Kal shoot the first load into his mouth. He backed off licking his head to consume it all. He rested his lips on the ridge of his head and licked the tip with his tongue. He listened to Kal as he passionately moaned. His body was going through contractions. Sean drained him, but he wanted more to swallow. "Give me more."

Kal interrupted his thoughts. "Stop, player, it sensitive right now." He pulled his swipe out. "I got another load."

"You can't take it, freak." Sean held him tighter and sucked more until Kal got a half erection. "You want to do me hard, now I'm gonna treat you, too!" When Sean was done, he wiped the cum off his lips with a finger then licked it. "Tastes good."

Kal stepped over to grab a warmer. He pulled it over himself, then laid on Sean's chest kissing him. "I feel your swipe rubbing on my ass crack."

Sean reached around Kal playing with the outside of his booty hole. "I want to feel your insides," he said, sensuously. He took grease sliding one finger into Kal, then two. He watched Kal moan softly. "I got to lube your hole."

"O-o-h, d-a-m-n, that feels good." Kal reached over to grease Sean's pole with a large amount! "You got a large swipe, do me slow at first. I just got off, but I am ready to go again!"

"You a tight boo-boo? I'll be slow to break you in. I'll get it open, trust me!" He whispered, tonguing him. He pulled Kal upward feeling his hand grab his swipe to guide it. He gently lowered him on it. He stared at Kal's face suddenly start to express emotion. He felt his fingers dig into his shoulders. "You like Daddy's swipe, don't ya? You got this dick?"

"A-w-w, yes." Kal fell to Sean's chest. He put his elbows on his chest and dropped his head forward, "o-o-h, y-e-s!" He let out a breath of air, weakly moaning, "f-u-c-k! It is long and big right now. Y-e-s! I got that dick."

"I got you," Sean moaned. "I'll break that ass in! When I am done, you will know you had some swipe. You gonna get a chocolate dick down."

"Do me," Kal murmured, softly, "it will fit. I want a dick down. I want to feel all that swipe, b-r-o-h-a." He squatted putting both his feet on the chair. Eventually, he felt Sean's upper legs hitting his ass. "Tap that shit, a-w-w! Take my sh-zit, big dawg, I want to feel those tight nuts hit my ass!" Kal moaned heavily, "o-o-o-h; o-o-o-h…"

Sean drove in deep, watching Kal's face light with such pleasure, "ride my trunk. You want to freak…freak!"

After riding on him for a while, Kal suddenly stood and turned around to guide Sean gently back in. He grabbed the chair's handles, then started to slowly bounce up and down. "That swipe feels so good!" He moaned louder. "Jag me while I fuck you with this tight ass!" He felt Sean grab his flopping swipe, "y-e-s, b-a-b-y, do me…"

"I love that tight hole you got," Sean groaned, he exhaled air onto Kal's back, "ride the elephant's trunk!" Sean held his swipe. "I'm getting ready to bust this shit inside of you; f-u-c-k…" He moaned and exhaled faster on his back. "F-u-c-k my trunk," Sean blew air harder onto his back. "Fuck this dick!"

"Yeah. Tap that shit! I want your shit!" Kalvin was in his pure pleasure zone. He could not stop!

"I am." Sean pushed him out of the chair onto the floor. "Arch that back." He turned and planted a knee on Kal's lower back. "I got to work this. You ain't been fucked right. I'll give you a proper dick down!"

"I need a good fucking." Kal was moaning heavily. "Oh, fuck, brotha; o-o-o-o-o-h…"

Sean felt his hand reach back and push against him. "Give me that hand." He clapped Kal's hand on his back. "I told you I would dick you down. You won't want sex for a week."

"Fuck brotha, d-a-m-n! I needed some dick right now!" Suddenly, Kal exclaimed louder, "I'm going to cum…cum with me."

Sean's brain lost all sense of reality, he pulled harder on Kal's swipe. He forced Kal across the floor as he rode him now holding his neck. "I'm…I'm busting…" Sean said, climaxing. He moved around, he bent his head to bit on Kal's neck! Sean could feel his cum on his other hand. He felt Kal bouncing faster. His jaw instinctively held his neck. "A-w-w," he warmly moaned, "take this dick, Boo-Boo!"

* * *

It was a nice day out at Kay's place. I got up earlier to slide out on the porch to smoke.

Kay did not like it when I smoked. It was still dark and I forgot that Kal and Sean were out there last night. I did not even think about it; the table was never put back. I figured they would be in the second bedroom. The wind was pulling the air out.

"Unck, you're smoking a cigarette?" Sean's head stuck out of the warmer.

I looked back, "yeah, having one." I saw Kal's head appear, too. "You two were out here all night?" I looked surprised.

"Yeah."

I stood looking at the skyline, "the sun is coming up. Kay will be up in a moment." Once finished, I headed to the door. "I'll let you two be alone."

Under the warmer, Kal was holding Sean's morning erection. Sean had his fingers on Kal's booty hole. "Unck, you okay with this?"

"With what, Sean?" I heard this question from him before. "With what, Sean? You are Sean!"

"With me and Kal chillin. You know, chillin like dhis?"

"How can…," I was emotionally taken back so I had to clear my throat. I was buying a few moments of time.

"Unck, you okay?"

"Sean, I…I love you. How can I hate or judge what god made." I quickly brought the side of my hand across my eyes. "I have no problems here."

"Thanks, Unck," Sean grinned. "My mama did me wrong. I appreciate you being so cool about this; thanks for being you! That's my Unck, Kal." He gave Kal a peck on the cheek.

I could barely manage the words, "Y-e-a…Yeah, thanks."

* * *

The kitchen light came on, Kay was up. I went back inside, Kay was getting ready to make breakfast.

"I guess those two slept out there last night. Wonder what they did all night!" I teased.

"You mean Humpty-Horny and Freaky-Kal!" Kay chuckled. "I told you they would like each other."

"Yeah," I slightly laughed. I stood behind Kay sliding her sweats down and running a finger over her clit. "Give me a shot of the shit. All this matchmaking you are doing is making my horny. I need to be match-made, also."

"Whitey," she paused to moan, "I'm trying to cook breakfast…"

"I'm trying to get breakfast," I slid my erection into her and pushed the pan off the burner. "Bend over, I want to tap it good!" I grabbed her to put her hands on the counter, then I reached up her sweatshirt playing with her hard nipples. I felt her juices already running out. Kay started moaning louder, then she knocked two cups and a pot on the floor. Glad the cups were plastic! "F-u-c-k, do me, baby."

* * *

Kal and Sean got up to peek through the window after hearing the noise. Kay had already opened the blinds a little on the window. Sean watched in the window. "Damn, Kal, Unck is in there gettin some!" He chuckled. "He tapping that sh-zit!"

Kal peeked, "fuck, you right. Sis fucking him just as hard." He laughed.

Sean grabbed Kal, holding his ass against his swipe, "I want to hit you like that! Harder than I did last night."

Kal smiled, "we do have to go in for breakfast, big dick Bob!"

* * *

Kal and Sean walked through the door. As Sean followed Kal, he noticed he was walking a little bow legged. "A little sore…"

Kay and I were sitting eating some eggs. "Get them while they are hot," Kay said.

"I'll get you some," Kal said, gesturing to Sean.

Kay got up to help. "Here's the eggs and here's some bacon. You okay, little brother?"

Kal smiled. "Yeah…"

"How you feeling, Unck?" Sean said, smiling ear to ear. He was sitting at the table.

I looked at his grin. "What? I feel fine."

Sean reached over to turn open the blind all the way. "How was per-breakfast?"

I turned beet red. I now just realized Kay must have opened the blinds a little when she entered the kitchen. I choked on the eggs. "A-h-e-m," I cleared my throat, "it was good, too."

Kay sat down with Kal. "What you two talking about over here?"

"Nothing, Kay," I replied.

She looked at me, then the boy, "yeah right, that big shit-eating grin on his face!"

* * *

We all had a good breakfast. Things were going so well, Sean and I stayed for three days to hang with Kay and Kal. It was a good time for all of us in Chicagoland. Sadly, all our joy was about to leave in a moment.

3. Unck Got Even

It was a rainy, dark night. The sun set and thunderstorms rolled through. It was a perfect night to go hunting. The officer which had pulled Sean over was in the best spot he could be for revenge; unfortunately he did not know this. I got lucky. My info guy came through.

The officer's record was tainted: basically he was stealing drugs and reselling them. He used a hard hand sometimes. He was the type of officer which had too many open cases for brutality. All were dealing with brothers. The writing was on the wall. After Sean, it would be his last.

* * *

"Hey, Jake," I greeted the bartender. My crew was located in the back parking lot. This is how good it worked: my info guy discovered his frequent visits to a bar. I personally knew the owner. He was a family friend. "How are things?" I loved Jake's oak bar.

"Hey, Whitey. I have not seen you for a while." Jake was polishing cups.

"It has been a minute. I see you remodeled a little bit." He had a beautiful Celtic bar.

"Business?" Jake inquired.

"Yeah. Loose ends. Business." I nodded my head. "It is at the end of the bar."

"Okay. Lights out?"

"Yeah. If you need it, I will send around the cleanup crew." I place a crumpled fast-food bag on the bar, "you never saw anything."

"I, laddie, old Jake always had poor vision," he slid the bag off the bar.

* * *

I sat down next to the man at the far end of the bar. "Hey…"

He stared at me with one too many in him. "Do I know you?"

"No, but I have seen you on the TV news. They always harass cops doing a good job. I am proud to meet you."

"Don't believe what you see on TV!"

"No, I don't. They are always lying to the public. Also, I want to thank you for helping my son. He is better now. Thank you, Officer White. He needed a good kick in the ass to straighten him out. You corrected his ways. Thank you. Police officer have a very hard job these days. People are so fast to say 'defund them', I don't believe that crap since all someone has to do is look at the high crime rate!"

"Who was he? I don't remember. Who are you?" He said, slowly, "I am a cop, you know."

"Yes, I know. I like your hard style. He is Black. Nice kid. You helped him. And, yes, you helped and protected. I am just saying: thank-you."

White looked at me. "I still don't know you. You know, I am a sergeant. What is this all about?"

"Yeah, I know. I understand your caution. I'm white; he is black. I adopted him." I switched the conversation off me. "So, can I buy you a drink?"

"Oh. Sure."

"Jake, please bring the officer a double of whatever he is drinking. I will take a beer."

"So, what was his name again?" Officer White asked.

I could tell he was a little too drunk. "Sean."

"How did I help? I honestly don't remember."

"Well, you showed him a good police officer. He was drunk the night you stopped him."

"Well, that is typical of them." He interjected.

"Yeah. But your good skills changed that."

"Glad I helped. What did I do?"

I was so glad he asked. "You put a club into his nuts, then tasered him when he pissed." I reached over to put my hand over his mouth. I pulled a locked knife, sticking him multiple times. The lights went out in the bar; I stuck him as many times as I could. He stared at me in the darkness. "This is what you get when you touch one of mine. Your wife and kids will be with you so you won't be lonely when you meet your maker. Your family is gone!"

He heard me, but could only stare. His head hit the bar. I held him so he wouldn't fall off the stool.

* * *

When the lights came on, I was by myself.

"Sorry, folks," Jake shouted. "The electrician will be here tomorrow to look at the fuse box. Everybody gets a free round on the bar." Jake walk down by me.

"Here Jake," I dropped a few C-notes. "You got the mess? Everything is good."

"I will do it myself, Whitey. Good to see you." Jake smiled, "I was starting to think you retired."

"Nice seeing you too, Jake."

* * *

I stepped out the rear door. "Excuse me, gentleman."

"Hey? Who are you? Jake just doesn't let anyone go out the back."

"My name is Williams. I asked Jake. I am with that van. Repairs."

"You're not Williams, I know your face! Your Whitey!" One man picked at his teeth. "I heard about you. I heard you killed more people than Ebola."

"I don't know anything about that. Must be another man," I smiled. Two shots in both of them. I helped load them into the van. "Okay, gentlemen, let's go. Now we got three bodies to make disappear."

G started laughing. "You something else…"

Kareem interrupted, " …damn, Whitey, what were you thinking? We stacking them up tonight. What is this whack Wednesday!"

"Where did they come from, Kadeem? One called me by my name. No witnesses. It is what it is. Besides you are: *Bill try the info guy!*"

"Oh, you got jokes now? They walk up on us, I was concerned about sending you a text or calling. I knew you could handle it." He spoke to G, "speed this up, brotha, 'cause one of these marks smells funky as hell!"

"Well, they are fucked now, no need to shower!" Greg joked. He rolled out driving the van.

"Remember you two not a word to anyone: meaning Kay or the kid!" I mentioned. These two were my right and left hand with the family business. They were my very trusted allies.

"Ooh, you ain't telling Kay," Kadeem stated. "What is going on 'cause inquiring minds want to know?"

"I don't want to worry her and I don't want the kid to say anything to anyone else. You two are my generals; I can't keep any secrets from you. If I did you would eventually figure it out anyways."

"Oh, so now I am not Bill-try-the-info-guy!"

"Kadeem, you are killing me here. Or, the stinky fucker back here is!" I laughed.

G interjected, "I would go with the stinky fucker! I can smell him, also!"

Kadeem replied to me, seriously, "the Street Reaper lives!"

* * *

The time came when Sean told me about what happen with the police officer. What happened to Sean burned in me. It was a hatred that would not go away: the po-po touched my boy! The Street Reaper came and left in the darkness.

4. County Jail Madness

Well, Sean was held in county. He was dealing with what the officer did and a D.U.I. charge. Lockup is a whole new world for a person. The den of thieves!

* * *

The jailer walked to Sean's cell front. "Hey…" he paused. "You want a shower?"

"Yes, I have been in this holding cell for seven days! What gives? I'm smelling ripe!"

Sean jumped up from his bunk, his swipe bounced around in his boxers so he grabbed the fly. He didn't want his swipe to fall out. "When am I going?"

"We have had a lot of men coming in over the past two weeks, we're trying to figure out what to do with all of them," the jailer replied, "I'm making a round. I'll be back in about ten minutes. Be ready. *Whitey sends a blessing.*"

Sean just stared for a second. "Awe, I will, I will take the shower; for sure!" He smiled. "You helping me out right now?" Sean thought to himself, *like what do I got to do to get ready! Unck sends his blessing?*

The jailer got Sean's sizes. "I'm helping because the smell in holding is getting stronger each day."

Sean waited for him to return. The moments seemed like hours. When the jailer said the name 'Whitey', he knew he was talking about his Unck. Yet, he was scared to trust anyone. "Finally, out of this cell," he mumbled. The concrete box was getting to him.

"Let's go," the jailer unlock his door.

Sean was surprised he did it without putting cuffs on him, "you didn't cuff me?"

"I am now. I told you I am a friend." The jailer loosely cuffed him. "In here, we learn who the assholes are pretty quick! If you don't give me any crap, I won't give you any crap!"

"Yes, sir. But, you said 'Whitey'. Who is he?"

* * *

The showers were placed on opposite walls in a line about six foot apart. They looked like cages. The door of the cage was visually wide open. This is how the jailers kept track of a men. In lockup, there is no privacy, right down to seeing a man's swipe!

In the intake section, it was hard not to be somehow in their eye sight. Sean's cell had a camera facing it. He could not even shit without being watched. If he got out of bed with a hard swipe, they could see it. He could not even jag himself. It was annoying to know they always saw everything. After seven days, he needed to satisfy his urge.

Most of the showers were empty. Yet, the one straight across from him was not. Sean did not care. He was just happy to not have a camera pointing at him! He did not have a choice which shower he was placed in. He badly wanted a shower. Yet, now his urge was persistent.

Once the jailer left, Sean started to wash. He heard the stories of men saying that a man should never shower naked. Other men would watch; those types. However, he only had a smaller brother in the other cage. *Hell, he thought, my boxers are all wet around my ass and swipe. Anyone could see through them!* As he washed, he could feel the wet cloth siding easily on his meat. I'm taking them off, he thought.

Sean didn't know it, but while he peeled off his soaked boxers; the brother was watching. The brother glanced out of the corner of his eyes pretending not to look. Sean's body infatuated him! Sean's stomach was flat with ripples of muscles on it. His nuts had that tight look. He had little body hair. The brother even noticed his nuts had no hair.

As the brother watched, Sean turned toward him to hold the bars of the shower door. As he lifted his left leg to get it out of the boxers, his nuts pushed on his swipe. It fell to the right bouncing on his other leg. It looked like it was half hard. The same thing happen when Sean lifted his right leg, but this time he had to shake his foot since the wet underwear wouldn't immediately slide off. This caused his swipe to bounce around more. Sean's urge started again.

"How you be?" The smaller cat in the shower across from him asked. He had thin, long dreadlocks that hung about neck level. He turned a little and washed his ass toward Sean's direction.

Sean did not miss this. "I'm good; finally. Seven days without water." Sean glanced his way again, then looked toward the shower. He noticed he was cut, thinner, and had little body hair, too. He lusted when he saw him wash part of his ass. His swipe started to lengthen more.

"Heard that! They got this placed filled and then some!"

Sean's mind was on something else. He went without sex for seven days. Sometimes, in the holding cell his swipe would get semi hard and drip fluids. He did not want anyone in the jail to see it. His mind focused on his needs. The hot water excited him. Hell, he would pull himself in the morning, go out to have sex twice, then come home to jag once more. This was just Sean.

Every morning when he awoke, his swipe was hard as hell. He had wet spots on his lower belly. He thought about Kal and Zak sometimes. He was experiencing more uncontrollable erections during the day. How do you hide thirteen inches? He did not want the jail staff looking at him.

There were times when his swipe would grow until hard. His head would drip fluids, sometimes it would get creamy. He would stand at the toilet like he was pissing. He was really massaging the head of his swipe hoping to ejaculate. He did not want to get caught so he did it as inconspicuously as possible. Then, he would hear a noise which stopped his concentration.

In the shower, he could feel his swipe start to feel heavy and grow. After he washed under his foreskin, his head would not retract. He had so much sexual tension built up, he didn't realize he was trying to attract a mate. At this time, his swipe was always swelling and dripping fluids. *Fuck*, he thought, *I want jag!*

He could not help what was natural. Usually, he liked the sexual tension when it built in him: the sweet anticipation of his swipe lengthen at a party with friends. Sean would look at the guests lusting at their bodies hidden under their clothes. He could feel the heaviness in his pants. It turned him on.

Yet, county was different. A man not having any type of sex could not hide his horniness. He started to get embarrassed when the white jailers would come to his cell. They could see his natural half hard swipe bouncing around in his boxers. He knew he had wet spots on his boxers.

As he showered, his swipe naturally lengthened another inch. His sexual tension was showing. When he cleaned his foreskin again, his penis head remained permanently out. It hung at nine or ten inches. He knew right there he was getting an uncontrollable erection! He tried to get Kal and Zak out of his mind. He wanted to pull it, but he had the guy in the other shower. He did not want him to see.

It was like the jailer purposely put them across from each other to stop them from having sex with themselves. His swipe grew more. The need to jag his swipe outweighed the brother looking. He looked down, he knew his body. The urge was very strong. He knew he was passing fluids.

He tried to figure out how to inconspicuously do himself. Then he noticed the brother would watch him now and then. His gaydar kept lighting in his brain. He wanted to bust so bad. There was something to this brother. Was it his tension? His soft meat normally hung at six to seven inches, now it stayed at ten and his head showed. He kept holding it in his hand while he showered, but this made it worse. It felt so good to just hold it.

Sean took the razor to shave. He had to get his mind off mating somehow. He soaped his face and gently shaved under the hot water. Once done with his chin, he ran it over his center chest area to remove any new hair. He did not like body hair.

Yet again, he noticed the brother was watching him. His gaydar took over. He did not care. He soaped his nuts to gently run the razor over them and the insides of his legs. He held his swipe head in his hand to pull it downward so he could shave above his penis. He shaved around his shafted to square it up. He only wanted a small patch. Finally, he ran it over the top of the remaining hairs to shorten them.

When he was done, his swipe filled out to eleven inches. Holding it to shave made it grow. He wanted to stroke it. Again, he noticed the brother was watching. This made him even more horny. His gaydar was swimming in thoughts each time he notice the brother watching. He was entering his pleasure zone just by being watched. His swipe was swelled, it did not hang loose anymore. It climbed to a full twelve inches. It stood out.

Eventually, the brother made small talk. "You okay over there?" He asked, as he glanced at Sean. He watched his pipe as it pointed straight out. He noticed when they started talking, Sean lost some of his erection. His foreskin retracted a little bit over his head. He could see Sean was horny!

Sean smiled a little, "Man, I ain't had it for a minute!" He noticed the brother had a half hard swipe so he took a chance. He stood looking out the shower door to see if any jailer was around. "When was the last time you got it in? I got to jag." As he spoke, he held the end of his swipe in his hand to massage it. Sean was sexually frustrated!

"I'll watch for guards, do what you do." The brother looked both ways, knowing the only way they would come in was by the security door which they slammed every time.

Once Sean heard that, he knew the brother wanted a show. Sean turned away and grabbed the washcloth. He hit it fast. He did not care if the brother watched, he just wanted to get off! "O-o-h," he moaned, as he held it in the washcloth to get it all soapy!

He was now like a two-minute brother, he had to release. He leaned against the side wall of the shower to look at the brother. His washcloth dropped and he began to pound himself with his hand. When he busted, he noticed the brother watched him. "O-h…o-h, damn!" He arched his back sticking his groin out so it was fully exposed.

As he unloaded, he grabbed the shower door facing the brother fully. His body uncontrollably shook as his muscles twitched. Once done, Sean stood there shaking his swipe. His swipe hung at ten inches. A swipe always hangs longer for a while after cumming.

He want to pull it again, but the jailer came back, "We're looking for two men to put into our old section of the jail. We're rebuilding back there. Will you go? You seem to be quiet. Otherwise, you may be in the holding cell for four to five more days. It is an eight-man cell, but there are only two bunks in it."

"I don't want to be in holding. I'll go!"

"I have to find someone else."

Sean responded, "how about him, he seems to be smooth. We were just chatting while waiting for you." Sean gestured to the shower across from his.

The jailer did not know what happened moments before. Sean watched the brother do the same to get off. However, he slid a finger into his booty to work it while he jagged. Sean, for sure, did not miss it! His gaydar flashed like a po-po car pulling a brother over.

"Okay, this will save some time. You two cool? It's the old part so I don't want any problems!" The jailer looked at both of them. They agreed. He stared at Sean, talking quietly, "I told you, Whitey sends his regards."

* * *

When they got to the cell, it was half dismantled on the inside. The guard asked them if they needed anything from the cart. Sean listened to the brother ask for some lotion to put on his skin. Then ask for some grease that was in small tubes, like ketchup packages that you would get from a store. "I need some toilet paper, toothbrush, and paste, too."

Sean followed, asking for the same.

"Hey, take what you need." The guard was trying to be nice since he knew they were in the old jail. He also knew Whitey. The guard told them he might not be back for a while so he gave then clean boxers, T-shirts, socks, wash clothes, towel, and more soap. "It looks pretty bad in here, but everything works."

They got books off the cart, too. His new celly only wanted a thin page book. Sean got three books that were thick. This would give him something to read. Also, he wanted them in case the brother gave it up. He was smaller, with the books he could jack up his ass by putting them under knees. He noticed his new celly had a firm ass that conspicuously displayed itself.

Eventually, the jailer left.

* * *

It was hot in the cell area so Sean removed his orange jail jumpsuit to walk around in boxers. Sean watched the brother spit out a lighter as he took off his orange jail suit. As Sean watched his celly his penis was pushing hard against the fly of his boxers. He asked for medium shorts, but the jailer gave him a small pair that were stretched.

His nuts pushed his swipe into the fly's opening which caused it to pull apart showing his shaft. He was so horny, but he didn't want to say anything. Jagging once didn't really do much for him, he wanted to get off good! Yet, he was still sizing up the brother. He did not want a drama queen. Sean walked around like an elephant with a trunk, but he also was trying to be cool. He thought he could finally jag at night under his blanket without anyone knowing.

Surprisingly, he watched the brother go to the toilet, strip, and push out a balloon from his booty. He grabbed the book with very thin pages to tear a page out. He rolled two joints. Sean now knew why he had the lighter. The brother went by the shower where there was an air vent pulling air from the cell. He exhaled into the vent, then invited Sean over, "you want some?"

"Sure." Sean did not know he was smoking weed with formaldehyde sprayed on it. He was grateful that the brother gave him something to take the edge off in this nothing ass place. He was so horny that he hope this would stop his erections, but it did not. Sean knew his half hard swipe was visible. He tried to hold his fly closed with one hand so it would stop showing. But, as he smoked; he forgot to do it.

The brother stood in the one-man shower. Sean's penis head made a print on his boxers. Sean stood by its opening. When he stretched into it to blow the smoke toward the vent, his upper shaft poked out of his fly. He didn't notice the brother watching it.

Sean respected that he trusted him, but he was still so horny. He remembered watching him slide a finger into his booty. It turned Sean on just to think about it. It was the sexual tension built up in him. All he could think about was sex. Being around this other guy was not helping. Sean's gaydar could sense it in him, but he did not want to move too fast.

Sean sat down, "it is so hot in here. We just got out of the shower and I'm all sweaty."

"Me too," the brother agreed. "It might be the weed."

"I appreciate that you turned me on to some."

"Cool; you seemed like you could use it."

Sean though about taking another shower, but decided differently. "I'm gonna wipe down with a washcloth really quick, then put some lotion on." Sean took a chance and pulled his boxers off. His swipe bounce back and forth on his legs. *Men get horny not being able to nut!* Sean stepped over by the toilet to piss. He noticed the brother watched him.

"Why don't you just take another fast shower?"

"I thought about that, but my mohawk will dry out."

Talking with him and wiping down frustrated him more because it was turning him on. His gaydar was flashing. The weed high he was enjoying had his mind turning elsewhere. He showed less self-restraint. His body was uncontrollably reacting to the brother's stares. It kept going into pleasure mode since it was deprived of sex. If he caught him, the brother causally looked away. Sean wiped lotion on his body. *Fuck*, Sean thought, *I got to get off.*

The brother politely moved to the other end of the cell. He was being respectful to give Sean some privacy. "I'll lotion up over here."

Sean looked back occasionally, he noticed he was still looking now and then. He watched the brother open almost all the grease packages squeezing them into a cup then mixed lotion into it. Sean watched him grease himself, this made him more excited. They both stood there naked. His stares gave Sean another full erection.

He turned sideways so the brother could get a full view. He knew the brother could see his swipe, but he had to take a chance. *Maybe he would be willing to at least jag me*, he thought. As he wiped down, he would occasionally pull on his meat. When he wiped his nuts, he thrust his waist outward. He kept stroking his swipe while he cleaned his nuts and inner legs. "I got to hit myself, again." Sean whispered. "Sorry. I'm just horny. Maybe I need to use the shower again." Then, he got a surprise.

The brother stepped over, "let me get your back; you missed some spots."

"Okay, thanks." Sean was loving it. His erection was producing precum. He wanted to jag while he was doing it; to be touched by another man excited him. The high produced a more intense feeling as his celly did it. The brother ran a hand over one of his booty cheeks, then apologized for doing it. "It's okay, it happens," Sean assured him. When Sean turned around after he was done, the brother could see his full erection was wet.

"I see you're ready for actions." The brother spoke softer.

"Yeah; seven days without it. Why don't you touch it."

Sean's head was a purple-reddish color. Against the background of his dark meat, it showed! Sean didn't say anything, but he pulled on it a few times. He held onto his head with his hand because it felt good. Yet, it seemed the brother was reluctant. "I'm gonna put my boxers on," he was getting ready to cover his hard swipe.

"Before you do, we'll oil this part, too," the man was toying with him. He massaged Sean lower belly, swipe, then rubbed his nuts. "You got some big, tight nuts." He lusted at Sean's groin; it was on fire. His balls stood out, swollen. "You have been in that holding cell too long," the brother teased.

Sean's brain was already in its pleasure spot. His natural needs to have sex took over.

More juices followed out of him. When the brother touched his dick, he could feel contractions. As a man, his needs to ejaculate sperm were always now on his mind. He knew the brother saw his precum ooze out of the opening of his penis head. Hell, jism was hanging an inch off the swipe now.

Sean watched the brother turn and backed up to slide his hard swipe into him. Sean started to thrust it harder, but the little brother stepped away. He almost ejaculated at that moment. "What are you doing?" Sean asked, surprised.

"What are you doing? You are too big. Slide it in slow, I never took anything that long."

"Okay…okay," Sean wanted to run his Mississippi black snake into him, but he didn't want to hurt him. He was a tight booty brother like Kal. Some brothers never loosen up after being continually fucked. It's like they got extra booty muscles. "Sorry, I did not mean to harm you." Sean started with one finger, the brother tensed up, "relax…" he said, softly, slowly rubbing his back, "…arch your back and stick out your booty." Sean walked him to the lower bunk telling him to rest his hands on the mattress. "Relax, arch your back down, it will go in easier." He slid in a finger from both hands, then gently pulled his booty apart.

The brother watched Sean's fluids dripping off it. "I see you want to fuck. You horny as hell," he stopped to moan, "o-o-o-h, it feels so good. Even your fingers are long."

"You want to fuck. I want to fuck!" Sean stated.

"Ya, I do with the right man. I need to be fucked." The smaller brother kept going erect, then falling as he felt Sean's fingers.

"Man, I'm so horny for booty! I can be the right man!" Eventually, the brother loosened. Sean noticed the brother had sperm hanging off his dick. He knew he was treating him right. "I'll slip my head in slowly." He greased himself good to just slide in his swipe head. The brother started the shake. He started to climb away. "Easy…I got you." He stood there holding him so he couldn't move off his swipe. He didn't want him to change his mind. Sean was running on his natural, basic needs now.

74

"I'm tight!" The brother exclaimed. "Like a virgin! You are long." He started rocking slowly on Sean's swipe head. He started sliding off him, then thrusting him back in. Eventually, Sean's swipe head slid smoothly. He only was taking three inches of thirteen!

Sean wouldn't release his grip, he wanted to mate! "See, it's going in. I will do it slow." He wanted to fuck like a brother. Like a guerrilla. It was that heightened sex cycle he had which would take over after long periods without sex! His testosterone was spiked. He never took it as too much arousal or sexual energy, he was horny and it was time to have sex!

As his animal instincts kicked in out of lust, he felt the brother start to pull away, again. It wasn't about love for him, it was his need to mate. He didn't want to hurt him, but he needed to fuck. His nuts were already turning dark purple from not ejaculating. "Where are you going, get on this dick." Sean held him, but went no deeper.

"You're at my spot, it takes time to get past it." The brother reached back moaning. "I love your dick." It was a moment for him, too. He was horny and needed to be fuck! He tightly grabbed Sean's nut sack knowing he had him. He'd grip his swollen balls tighter and pull him back. If Sean acted right, you know, did not try to ram him, he would not pull hard. Even the biggest man would bow down or suffer the pain in his testicles. Yet, he didn't realize Sean thirsted for shit like this.

When the brother tightly held his nuts, as a thug he respected it. He felt him push his balls back, "I got you bitch!" Sean felt some pain, "don't let go of my nuts go, I want to fuck your way!" He felt a squeeze. "I told you I got you, hold my nuts to guide me! Pull on them to go forward and push them back to stop." As his slid it further, he knew it was only in five inches. The brother held his nuts tight as he worked his swipe slowly. Eventually, he opened up. Sean felt it on his swipe, suddenly he smoothly slid in.

Sean slid almost all his swipe in, "arch your back, stop raising it like a camel! Spread your legs more. Hold onto my nuts, my cool 'cause I got it!" He felt for a moment his grip tighten on his nut sack, "aww…that feels so good." Sean almost busted at that gesture! Sean put one leg on the bunk, "you got this Mississippi black snake!"

The brother spread his legs out some more, then back up on Sean's swipe taking it all.

He took it slowly, moaning, "o-o-o-h, my booty." The brother's swiped had more sperm dripping. "I got to pull myself!"

As soon as he started, Sean felt his booty tighten. It turned him on more, he entered his pleasure zone. His brain took over, his couldn't stop. He started developing sexual flush on his chest. He laid on his back and grabbed the brother's chest. He opened his mouth to gently bite his neck. "Awe…" he moaned, drool ran out his mouth, "a-w-w, I'm gonna nut!" He held his smaller body thrusting himself into him faster. Sean's upper leg muscles glistened with light sweat. The brother's booty tightened then relaxed with each thrust.

"I feel your clamp on my neck. Why are you biting me?" He felt the saliva drip from Sean's mouth running down his neck. He felt Sean squeeze him tighter getting ready to ejaculate. He could feel Sean's swipe thicken in him. He laid there as Sean's two arms reached past his shoulders two rest on the bunk. He pulled harder on himself which caused his booty to tighten more. "Do me baby, give me that dick! Tell me what you're doing; tell me you're gonna cum!"

Sean moaned, he released his jaw from his neck. He was pounding air out his noise by the brother's ear, "I got me a bitch, I'm cumin." He couldn't hold back, "Take this shit!" He felt himself getting ready, so he bit his neck a little harder, "h-m-m…! I ain't fucked in so long." His ejaculation started. If anyone was standing behind watching, they would have seen the area behind his nuts uncontrollably spasm as his orgasm flowed.

"Do me, baby! Pump that swipe into me. Talk dirty to me, I'll take it all now; hard. I feel you in me." The brother wiggled around as Sean thrust himself into him as fast as he could. "All that dick in me…A-w-w, it feels so good!" He started murmuring as he felt Sean's swipe pounding his booty hole. His booty tightened, then loosened. He reached back with one hand trying to push Sean back.

"Get that hand back," Sean grabbed it and held it on the center of his back. "Bust so I can feel that booty hole tighten!" Sean stated, grunting, "Come on, bitch, fuck harder."

"Okay, do me like a bitch! Take that hole." The brother moaned, quietly, "Shit, shit. A-w-w-w…A-w-w-w…"

Sean moved in to bite his neck, again, "A-w-w…" He busted again. He felt his penis pulsate as the cum flowed, "I'm busting!" Sean finally released some of the anxiety built from his sexual tension. He lasted eight seconds as his muscle uncontrollably pulsated forcing his sperm into the brother's booty hole. He felt the brother bust at the same time. He kept rocking it into him to help him finish.

"H…u…h…h…h," Sean moaned, breathing heavily. "O…o…h, you feel so good."

They both felt each other as they relaxed. Sean stopped biting his neck. He was like a cat holding his mate. Sean's swipe started to return to its normal level. The brother's did too. The brother tried to pull out Sean's dick.

"Stop, it will go easier if you let me get softer, then slide it out!" He felt him comply so Sean held him. "Let this swipe get soft!" Sean's thirteen inches relaxed. His penis head went under his foreskin as he gently slid it out. *I want to fuck again!*

* * *

Over time, the jailer came back with their supper. The trustee was helping and talking with Thay; Sean learned the brother was named Lil-Thay. He could see they knew each other. Sean stepped over to ask the jailer to turn up the TV, "hey, can you put a few notches on it." When the jailer turned his back to adjust the volume, he watched Thay slide the brother a joint.

"If you need supplies," the new jailer said, "the trustee will give them to you."

Sean stepped down to get his supplies. He was so high he forgot about his underwear; holding the fly closed. Thay talked to the jailer to thank him for being nice. The trustee watched Sean's fly open.

"Here, I'll give you different shorts, those are a little tight," he smiled. "I'll be back later with cleaning supplies; it's dusty back here."

Sean quickly grabbed his fly to hold it closed. "Sorry." He was a little embarrassed. His swipe still hung down in one of the legs of his boxers. It was still thick after having sex.

* * *

In the evening hours, the jailer came back with the trustee. The jailer did a security check while leaving Dewayne, the trustee, with the cleaning supplies. He locked him in the runway in front of the cell.

"How you doing?" Dewayne asked, noticing Thay walked a little bow-legged. "You okay?"

"Yea, I'm good. Nothing like that. He is just a long, big brother," he whispered. "You know my tight booty."

Sean got up to help clean. He approached the bars to grab the mop to side it in between the bars. He still had on the same underwear. As he grabbed the mop handle, his swipe shaft opened the fly, again.

Thay grabbed the mop telling Sean that Dewayne was cool. He introduced him, "This is my friend."

They made small talk. Sean could see it in Dewayne, too. His gaydar went on. As they talked, Dewayne joked that his shaft showed in the fly. "Change your shorts." Sean felt his fingers reach though the bars and flicked the end of his swipe a couple of times.

Dewayne asked Thay for a light. He lite the joint to pull a hit then placed it in Sean's lips.

He casually watched Sean's swipe hang longer. It grew about an inch after he flicked it. He reached through doing it again.

Thay took the baby powder, poured some in a sock, and shook it around. He sprayed chemicals everywhere. Sean stepped closer to the bars watching Dewayne stare at him and his swipe. "You are making it harder!"

"Yes, I see! I like how it slides down the leg of your boxers."

Sean stroked himself a few times. "Thanks for the cleaning stuff," he leaned a shoulder on the bars. He could feel he was getting heavy in his boxers, but he did not pay it much mind. As he talked, he moved one of his legs and shook his boxers to open up some room in the leg area.

"You're a long one," Dewayne commented.

"Yeah," Sean blushed a little. He pulled more on his shorts to bring the leg area further up. As he smoked, he could feel another uncontrollable erection. "Thanks for the hit." As Sean exhaled, he watched Dewayne slide to his knees to look at him closer. He started to play with his underwear.

Thay came over to rub Sean's booty with one hand and his stomach with the other, "let's get these off." Sean stood naked as Thay grabbed his tight nut snack to massage them with his hand.

"A-w-e," Sean moaned. He watched Dewayne play with his meat. As he enjoyed the high traveling through his brain, each one of Dewayne's touches sent a thrill across his swipe.

Dewayne was a scientist. He slid his foreskin back, then played with his head. Thay kept rubbing his belly and running a finger over his booty crack. Dewayne brought Sean's swipe through the bars to begin a blowjizzle. Sean shot quick. He could feel Dewayne roll his tongue, drinking it all down. Sean could barely take it, his swipe was so sensitive!

Thay watched Sean bust while he pulled on his nuts. "You good, brotha?" He touched the area behind his nuts as it spasm. "Get it all out!"

"Y-e-a-h," Sean moaned. "Y-e-a-h!" Sean grabbed the bars.

* * *

The evening closed in on Thay and Sean. Every now and then, he would feel his limp swipe. Sean sometimes pulled his foreskin back to run a finger on his head. It was still sensitive after his day with Thay and Dewayne. He watched Thay's ass as he move around the cell.

Thay started to get into his bunk, but he felt Sean's hand. He chose to lay with Sean for a while.

Thay slid the sheet back and took off his boxers. He parked his booty against Sean, then arched one of his legs. He laid Sean's swipe on his other leg. "That's better," Thay said softly. He could feel Sean's swipe grow from its seven-inch limp state.

Sean gripped him, kissing. "Let's fuck one more time!"

5. Playing with Doctor Zak

Sean awoke early one morning listening to Thay lightly snore. The days were passing faster now. With no one else around them, and being locked in the cell area to fill the boredom, they fucked. Sometimes Sean would jag Thay off to just watch him cum. Other time Thay would give Sean a blowjizzle, after he came in his mouth he would lick on his swipe until it went limp.

* * *

Sean was lying on his bunk having daydreams of when Zak and him had first had sex. He pulled the sheet over himself to use the toilet. As he walked back to jump in bed, he just let his swipe bounce around, hitting his legs. He notice Thay lay in bed with an erection as he slept. Sean dozed off dreaming.

* * *

Sean was in the locker room drying off from his shower one day. He had not had sex with anyone for a while. Even though he pulled himself, his sexual tension was growing. It was just not the same as someone else touching his body.

Surprisingly, he noticed Zak walk over to open a locker next to his. Zak knew where Sean's locker was located so he decided to take an empty one near his. They had hung out a little before this, both knew the other was gay.

Sometimes, Sean would hit on Zak for sex, but Zak didn't seem to be interested. Yet, now his tension was building.

However, the more Zak was around Sean, the more his thug thing did not offend him. You know, Sean had that side! Zak started to realize this was just how Sean acted.

"Hey Zak, how are you?" Sean glanced at his ass under the towel. He liked Zak, they were becoming better friends.

Being around someone else gay always made Sean feel more comfortable. At times, being with a cool gay brother he would get one of his uncontrollable erections just from being happy. It was not like he had to fuck, he was just in his comfort zone. Sean did not realize that his thug side offended Zak. He was gentle, too. Truth be told, this was just Sean.

"I'm good," Zak replied, "I thought I would catch a college basketball game today and relax." Zak was careful not to show his desire of looking at Sean's body. He was amazed at his length, how his nuts pushed his shaft out making it swing as he dried off. He played with his own swipe under the towel, admiring Sean.

Zak looked at his chiseled chest! Sean was cut, he did not have a six-pack, he had an eight! Zak liked how his arms, legs and booty were perfect. He watched his uncut swipe bounce around over his nuts. Zak really wanted to fuck with him. Zak had that freaky other side in him.

Sean commented, "I was gonna to do the same thing. I got a little wine in my dorm room if you want to chill together and watch the game." As Sean dried himself, he pulled on his swipe with the towel as he faced Zak, he started to get the beginnings of one of those uncontrollable erections. He was feeling happy. His penis grew half hard, then it started to fall. Was he fishing?

Zak smiled innocently, looking at his semi-hard swipe. He began to lust wondering how long and hard it could really get. He could not believe Sean stood to his side barely covering it with the towel. "I'd like that. Maybe we could party a little." He watched Sean get dressed. He placed the towel on the wooden bench. Zak watched his semi-erection lay over his leg pointing at him. His foreskin had a little opening just showing a little of his penis head.

Sean pulled his cup up, then stood trying to push it all in. He turned to Zak, "we'll have a good time. And, I promise Zak, no funny stuff!" He chuckled.

Zak was already in lust mode. When he pulled his towel off, he now had an erection! His six inches of fatter swipe that was hard as hell. If he moved the towel; he played with it. He thought about what his mother said about people getting the wrong idea. "I got to get dressed, give me a minute!" He turned away from Sean since he didn't want him to see. He felt embarrassed about it.

Sean stepped over the bench. He stood there waiting. "Okay, no worries."

Zak glanced back at Sean, he watched him rub his swipe a few more times. He positioned his swipe into the cup better since it relaxed. If Zak ever did this, his mother would have corrected him. He was amazed at how Sean thought it was okay behavior. "Can I run to the washroom before we go?"

"Sure." Sean stood there watching Zak. He bent over to dry his feet. Sean stared at his ass. He stroked himself some more. He noticed his large nuts hanging between his legs and a swollen cock. He saw Zak was cut and his dick head looked like it was gonna stretch out so far that it would burst. His head was light-reddish.

Zak innocently put another athletic cup on to make his swipe hold tight against his body. "Okay, I'm ready," Zak replied, "Let me use the washroom." He stood there buttoning up his shirt. Zak was always a neat dresser.

He ran to the washroom as fast as he could. Once in a stall, he masturbated. He was dreaming about Sean. He took his other hand to play with his nuts and booty hole. He pictured Sean's swipe bouncing around. It did not take long, he was less than a two-minute brother.

* * *

In the dorm room, Sean immediately turned on the game. It was Michigan state! Zak sat in one of the chairs by the TV. He pushed on his penis when Sean was not looking. He didn't want him to think he was horny. He looked back now and then to watch Sean stand by his closet area.

"I got to switch out sweats. Thanks for coming. You want to step out?" Sean asked.

Zak replied, "no, I'm good. I'll watch the game." As he watched Sean turn a little to his side, he deceitfully watched him strip. He only slid on his black sweats. He was not wearing any underwear! If Sean looked, he would focus on the game. He watched Sean pull his meat a few times! He couldn't believe he did it so casually!

"I got to use the restroom," Sean relied, "you know; dorms."

Zak start thinking them thoughts. When Sean stepped out, Zak put one drip of Ecstasy into Sean's drink and busted open two Viagra tablets. He stirred it, then opened his cooler to pour some juice and wine into it. He knew Sean like to mix other juices with his wine. As, you know, that was Zak's sneaky freaky side.

When Sean came back, he noticed the wine cup, "You filled my cup? Thanks!"

"Yes, I put juice in there so it will not be too strong." He watched Sean drink it down.

"Thanks, I was thirsty. All the working out."

As time passed, Sean offered Zak half of a sandwich and a small bag of chips from the college cafeteria. Sean was just doing his daily chores in his room trying to clean a little and watching the game. "Just trying to neaten things so you don't think I'm a slob!" He felt excited to have Zak over; to chill with another gay brother. "That cup of wine hit me stronger than usual."

Sean was wearing his favorite pair of sweatpants, they were a little bigger on his waist since the elastic was worn. Yet, his swipe hung in them perfectly. The material wrapped around his meat. They would slide down most of the time, but he paid it no mind. His shaft would hold them up.

"Thanks for the sandwich. You okay?" Zak asked.

Sean saw him looking at his swipe, "sorry, it does that sometimes. It is one of those erections. Little Sean sometimes has a mind of his own." He laughed, "this is kind of embarrassing. I wasn't even thinking about sex!" Sean again laughed, enjoying his high.

"You do not have to be embarrassed. We are alone."

"I'm just happy to hang with a gay brother. You know, don't have to show my public image! It is just me, Zak. I'm just happy to be with someone like me." Sean was feeling a little guilty about it. "It just lengthens, it is not hard-n-all."

"No worries. I sometime have that issue, too."

Suddenly, the announcer said something on the TV. Sean stepped over reaching passed Zak. He grabbed the remote. His leg pressed on the back of Zak's arm and his swipe hit the side of it, "I want to hear that…This fucking thing; the batteries must be going dead!" He moved so fast, he lost his balance so he grabbed the desk with his other hand. When he bent over a little his sweats slid down, showing part of his ass.

Zak lusted at it hanging in his sweats. He felt his weight against him and his swipe rubbing on his arm. "Here, let me move a little," Zak slid the chair over and placed his other hand on Sean's lower back. He could feel the top part of his booty so he rested his hand just on the top of it.

As Sean tried to get the second game on the TV, Zak looked at his showing neatly shaven penis hairs. This was the closest he had been next to him. Zak smiled, "Okay. You good?" Zak watched his sweats slide down a little more. His shaft was holding them up.

"Sorry. I'm good. I must be a little dizzy from the wine. Maybe I need to eat."

Zak was in heaven, he loved this time with Sean. If Sean wasn't looking his way, he would rub on his harden penis, then push it between his legs. Zak stared at Sean's shaft, he could see it swinging around in his sweats. It was so beautiful. "You like sports?" He watched as Sean would wiggle his leg, when he did it his swipe would rub on his sweats.

"Yeah, I just wanted to catch that." He turned the TV down. "I like basketball." Sean then stepped behind Zak's chair, he put a hand on Zak's shoulder not even thinking about what he was doing.

"That's cool." Zak was infatuated! He loved that Sean did not take this as abnormal behavior. Like he had no clue his penis touched his shoulder. Zak was precumming in his pants, again.

Zak watched Sean bend over to pick through his dirty laundry. His black sweats slid half off his ass—again! When he stood, he pulled on the back a little. When he turned, Zak saw the top part of his penis. Sean pulled them up, but they kept sliding down. Zak's groin was on fire.

"Zak, I got to run to the bathroom again to piss," Sean said.

"Me, too! I'll come with you."

* * *

They both ran to the bathroom, no one was in there. Sean locked the entrance door, he noted that would keep anyone from coming in. "Some of these dudes got things about gay brothers." Sean stood over the toilet since there was only one urinal. He did not close the stall door.

Zak finished first so he washed his hands. He noticed when he looked in the mirror he could see into the stall. Zak watched Sean stand there with his penis and nuts flopped out laying just over his sweats. He loved how his penis head stuck out a little from his foreskin. He knew the Viagra was working. The Ecstasy had him high as hell.

When Sean was done, Zak stepped a little closer to the stall. "Sean, you have to maintain proper hygiene!" He notice he did not wipe his penis head with toilet paper. Zak's brain kicked in so naturally about the need to be clean.

Sean stopped, turning, "what?"

Out of instinct, Zak grabbed piece of toilet paper, "you should wipe your penis so you don't spread germs!" He loved it that Sean let him do it, his penis was so beautiful! He stared at Sean's beautiful black shaft with its veins clearly showing.

Sean looked, laughing, "man, that felt good. I am so sensitive right now. I don't know why." He thought this would be a good day to hit on Zak for some booty. "You sure don't have any trouble grabbing a dick, do you?"

They both dashed back to the dorm room. Zak took a drop of Ecstasy. Sean was curious about it so he gave him another one. "It will make you mind focus in more on whatever you are experiencing at the time." They both were high on the drops and wine.

The Viagra was getting to Sean's groin.

Once inside, Zak couldn't help but ask Sean the question. "You horny? I saw your penis head sticking a little out of your foreskin." He giggled. "It looks sexy."

"Always!" This caught Sean off-guard. "So now you're watching me." He smiled. "When I hit on you for sex, you didn't seem to want it. Why ask?"

Zak replied. "It is bouncing around in your sweats." He giggled again. "If you're horny, it's okay. I was just asking." *What a subject to get Sean focused on!*

"I'm just glad to hang out; you know, with another gay brother." Sean naturally gave Zak a gentle hung. "I get horny some times, but I don't really feel it right now."

Zak smiled, feeling Sean's swipe pressing on him when he did it. "I guess I misread you. You got that thug thing which scared me, but I see you're also gentle."

Sean smiled. He put his hands on his waist, causing his sweats to somewhat slide down. His penis hairs were once again exposed. "Zak, I like freaky sex! But, I want to work with the person I am with. I guess I'm more open; that's me. That is the thug in me! I felt your hand on the top of my booty. I took it as two gay brothers chillin. You wiped my swipe. We touch each other; our swipes get hard, but that don't mean we have to have sex. I'm just excited to be with you."

"But, your sweats," Zak replied. "Your man hairs are showing. When you bent over a few times, your butt was showing."

Sean looked down at himself. He pulled his sweats up a little. "I guess they are. Sorry, if it offended you. I can slip on my other pair with my cup. I guess I'm so comfortable wearing these in my room I didn't think about them sagging." Sean joked, he pulled them up to his belly button, "I could wear them like this!" He saw Zak looking at his swipe again, "I see you looking!" He smiled. "No worries, I look at other men, too. Zak, I'm chillin!"

Zak damn near fell out of his chair. He could not hide his own horniness anymore. "Okay. I got it. You don't have to change. It is your dorm room, not mine. I like freaky sex, too. I bet you walk around naked in here by yourself."

"Yes, I do."

"When you feel horny alone in here, do you masturbate a lot?"

"Sometimes I jag as many times as I can to where myself out. I bet you be doing the same thing, you're just not telling."

"Yeah, I do sometimes. I like your body, I want to do some freaky stuff to you." Zak giggled. "I should not have said that. It was way out of line. The wine has got to me!"

Sean smiled, letting his sweats go, "you were not out of line. If you do not tell me, then how will I know? I'm about anything once!" He chuckled, embarrassed. "May be that was out of line!"

"What kind of things are you into?" Zak asked. While Zak talked, he became more comfortable with Sean so he touched his groin as he readjusted his pants. Zak was happy he now had Sean talking about sex. The announcer on the TV said something. "Hold on," Sean grabbed the remote standing next to Zak holding his shoulder with his other hand. Sean bent over a little.

Zak once again put his hand on his lower back. He could feel the top part of his ass. "What? What is going on with the game?" Zak was staring at Sean's penis hair.

Sean cheered a little at the TV. When he did this, his swipe bounced in his sweats. "Colorado won!" He put the remote down. "Zak, Colorado won!" Sean didn't notice, but after he was done celebrating, his movement caused the top of his shaft to show a little. Zak started to move his hand away, "you can leave your hand there!"

"Okay."

Sean smiled, "I'm chillin with a gay brother. I'm in my comfort zone! I can be me and you can be you! You can touch my body. If I get horny and you do not want to have sex, I'll hit the bathroom to jag. We don't have to have sex, but when you're gone I'll probably jag three times!" Sean joked, "and, I do like walking around naked in here." He trailed off in laughter, not paying any attention to his sweats.

"See, you're so open about sex," Zak paused. "You really gonna masturbate like that, three times?"

"What? Why not! I ain't gonna lie, I'm a horny brotha." Sean reached into his sweats watching the TV. He pulled on himself a few times. "It feels good!" He started laughing from his high.

Zak again almost fell over as he did this next to him. He could see his long penis and his hand playing with it. "I got needs, too. I'm scared to say anything! You; you are so open about it. You are barely wearing any clothes."

"Zak, I took my T-shirt off because it is hot in the room." Sean paused, smiled, then said, "Zak, just say what you're thinking. I'm cool. If I don't agree, we can still be friends. You can be natural around me! Are we okay here, you and me?"

"I like your body...; I'm just going to say it!" Zak paused, because he felt Sean push himself against his back. This infatuated him. "Okay, I'll say it. You want to play doctor? I like masturbating brothers. I like to be the boss and watch them cum. It turns me on. I be thinking about it, like with you. I'm studying to be a doctor. I like to play a sex doctor." He paused, "I should not have said anything." Zak got quiet. He started to feel embarrassed.

"So, you got freaky thoughts, too. I like that." Sean picked him out of the chair from behind. "You need a hung, you're sexually stressed. You can play doctor, I'll be your patient."

Sean slipped his sweat down so he stood naked, only wearing socks. "Okay if I keep my socks on?"

"You sure? I'd like that." Zak started to talk more clinical. "Sure, let's have a little more wine and juice."

Zak noticed as they stood there having their drinks to watch the end of the game, Sean's penis stretched all the way out to thirteen- and one-half inches. He had a full erection, then it started to decline. "Have you had a sexual checkup? Your inner part examined? Gay men should do this, you know. I see your penis works okay!"

"No, I haven't done that." He chuckled. "I think I should. I be ejaculating a lot, do you think I jag too much?"

"No, it is normal for younger men to masturbate." Zak turned rubbing Sean's man hairs. "I like how you shave." He looked at Sean's swipe. "How long is it really?" Zak kicked his shoes off and let his pants fall. Zak loved his touch, his big hands felt so good.

"I'm naked, I think I need a checkup, Doctor Zak. You know, make sure I'm okay! I mean everywhere. Can we do that?"

"Okay," Zak giggled. Zak's penis was hard. He touched Sean's penis a few times. "When I cum, it stretches to thirteen plus inches. Is that okay, Doc?"

"Good." He gently pulled his foreskin back so he could rub his penis head. "I want to see it! It looks a little dry. It needs to be oiled." Zak pulled on his meat some more. "Do you have a ruler so I can measure for the record!" He watched Sean's penis bounce around. "You need a doctor to give you some attention!" He giggled.

"Okay," Sean replied, turning the TV down. He handed Zak a ruler and pulled on himself to make sure it was fully hard. "I think it is there."

"O-o-o, thirteen and one half," Zak noted. "Doc's penis is hard, too!" He measured himself.

"This shit is fun!" Sean stroked Zak swipe.

"I want to practice being a doctor."

"Okay," Sean smiled. He was high as hell.

"Get on the bunk on your fours so I can inspect your body." Zak watched him. His erection kept bouncing around. "I need some gloves. You got vinyl gloves?"

"Yes, in the bottom drawer." Sean's swipe now had two inches of fluid dripping. He felt Zak put a towel between his legs.

"I'm going to get you more excited." He gently slapped his nut sack with the plastic ruler.

Zak stood by Sean's head with his swipe in front of his face. "Okay; more excited? My swipe is already dripping."

Zak continued, "I'll collect your discharges on the towel. I can see it dripping." Zak rubbed on his shoulder, then reach over him to feel his back. Zak's penis rubbed on of Sean's shoulder. He looked down watching Sean look at it so he moved in front of Sean, "get on your elbows so I can better reach your lower back." He watched Sean comply and open his mouth, "suck on me while I check out your back."

Sean rolled his tongue swallowing it all. He sucked on it slowly. Sean felt Zak's hands moved slowly up his back and then grab his hair.

"You like Doctor Zak's penis?"

Sean made a 'aw-ha' sound as he sucked. He felt Zak grab his hair harder, so he sucked faster. Suddenly he felt Zak tense to start shooting cum. Zak's penis head swelled. Sean lick over Zak's penis feeling his body thrust sperm into his mouth. "Awe, that tastes good."

"Swallow it all," Zak moaned. When he was done cumming, he moved behind Sean. "I need you to arch your back to raise your booty. It makes a prostate check easier." He again gently spanked his nuts with the plastic ruler.

Sean complied, in pleasure, "okay, doctor; I like it when you hit my nuts with the ruler." He felt Zak pull harder on his nuts, then spank them some more. "O-h, that feels so good."

"That is to get you excited." Zak put one finger into some grease. "Spread your legs out. I want to feel your prostate. Are your nuts always this tight?" He saw that he liked him doing it. "When you masturbate, do you pull on them?"

"Y-e-s, y-e-s, Doctor Zak!" Sean was breathing heavily. "You can pull on them, too."

"Arch your back some more so I can see them better." As Sean complied, Zak pulled them a little harder. "I want to feel each one. I have to check these, too."

"Okay," Sean moaned. He clenched the blanket with his hands. He was loving it. His shit kept dripping precum. "Make sure my nuts are okay, Doctor Zak."

Zak notice Sean's body shake a little as he tugged. "Are you okay? I'm not pulling to hard?"

"N-o; you can pull h-a-r-d-e-r," Sean now laid his head on the bed and spread his legs out more, "is that better?"

"Yes," Zak gripped then harder, massaging each one, "I'm feeling for lumps. It is a little harder because you have an erection and they have pulled tight into your body." He pulled on each one to feel around. "Okay, they're good." He gently took his palm to massage them. "This will help." He grabbed Sean's erection pulling it back between his legs. Zak was drooling as he licked his lips with his tongue.

Sean had plenty of fluids dripping out. He watched it for a minute. Sean had another fluid discharge when he touched it. "That is good, you are having fluid discharges." With his other hand, he massaged his booty hole. "Turn a little toward me."

"Okay."

After Sean did it, he let his swipe go to get some more grease. He massaged Sean with his finger. Then, he grabbed Sean's swipe again from the back. "I'm seeing if you're having a good discharges out of you penis head. Usually, if a doctor massage a man's anal area it will help the flow. I am grabbing your testicle and rubbing the area behind your nuts to see if it is hardened, too."

"O-o-h," Sean moaned, "I don't know what you are doing...but," he moaned again, "man it feels great." He loved every one of Zak's gentle tugs on his nuts and his fingers gently squeezing the area behind his nuts. His finger in his ass just hit a certain spot which made Sean feel so good and so horny.

"I'm massaging your prostate. This will take a minute," Zak replied, passionately. "I want to see if you'll ejaculate. I have to arouse…" Suddenly, as Zak was massaging the area behind Sean's testicles, he felt a contraction. He watched his penis thicken and his head swelled a little. A good shot of fluids followed. Sean released precum and sperm into the towel.

Sean laid back a little more relaxing. "Okay, Doc," he whispered. "O-o-h, keep doing it, Doctor Zak."

Zak grabbed a wipe to clean Sean's penis head. He watched Sean reach his arms back laying on his chest to put his hand on his leg. "This will take a minute, I want to see if I can make you ejaculate when your prostate is massaged. I might have to rub your penis head with two fingers."

Zak could hear Sean breathe heavier. He started moaning. Zak's other hand gripped his testicles pulling them upward. He watched Sean's erect penis drip more. He could feel him have an involuntary contraction now and then. "Good."

"O-o-o, don't stop! It feels so good! I'm close, Doc!"

Zak felt Sean's testicles pull in tighter. "I need to hold your testicles upward and squeeze them." He observed three or four involuntary muscle contraction in the area behind Sean's testicles. He wiggled his finger somewhat faster in Sean's booty. "You need a good prostate massage! It will show your sexually ability to ejaculate."

"O-h," Sean murmured, "O-o-h. Keep doing it, Doctor Zak!" Sean was in pure pleasure right now. "I'll be your cum doggy." When Zak wiggled his finger, he could feel himself ejaculate fluids.

Zak watched Sean's penis bounce a little. The contractions flowed through his body. "I need to massage this area. My cum doggy needs a good strong discharge to release his sexual tension." Zak put his thumb on the area behind Sean's testicles.

"O-o-h," Sean whimpered. He move his hips back and forth a little as Zak did it. His finger in his ass felt so good, "Keep massaging me!"

Zak felt more involuntary contraction. He watched Sean's penis head shoot some sperm, "you're doing good, Sean, I'm almost done," he said softly. "You are letting out sperm now."

Sean just passionately moaned, "more; make me cream."

He watched Sean's horniness release his sperm without having his penis shaft touched. It turned Zak on so much, he was dripping out his own erection. He could tell Sean was at his peak. He grease his hand and pulled Sean's foreskin all the way back, "I have to examine your penis head; get you foreskin out of the way." He started massaging the bottom of his penis head with his thumb. He felt his penis swell to its full length.

Sean was now jagging Zak as he did his procedure. "A-w-e," Sean rocked. His body had harder contractions. His penis lifted up and down by itself as some drops shot into the towel. Then, more sperm followed flowing out to drip off.

Zak watched Sean keep having spasms. He watched Sean shoot into the towel. "You are doing good, sometimes gay men feel very sexually excited during this examination."

"I want to masturbate so hard right now. I'm too excited."

"That is normal."

"I'm okay?"

"I need to see you have a strong ejaculation." Zak started to play with Sean long hard penis. He watched Sean's penis bounce around so he squeezed Sean's nut sack.

"Is that okay, Doctor Zak?" He felt Zak's swipe dripping on him.

"Yes," Zak bent over to suck his swipe. "As a doctor, I have to simulate you with oral sex." He began pulling his own penis. Zak was like an animal, he kept sucking and sucking. Sean was in heaven. He felt Zak bend his swipe back to suck it. Sean started to lift his booty more, his body took over.

Zak listen to him moan. He sucked harder. He felt Sean pulsate in his mouth. Cum dripped out of Zak's mouth. Zak immediately sprayed cum on Sean's leg.

* * *

Sean woke in the bunk pulling the sheet off himself, his swipe was fully erect with wet juices. He grabbed a towel to place it on his stomach. He started to jerk off. He watched his dick start to shoot out cream on the towel.

The jailer yelled, "breakfast."

6. Getting to Know Friends of a Feather

Thay and Sean were stuck in county together. Some days dragged, others moved along. They both got to know each other better, yet it was jail: a man may tell another anything. Most want to be this great successful lawbreaker. Few were truthful.

* * *

Sean and Thay were sitting in the cell playing dominoes or bones. Thay won another game. He had a few comments on how easy it was to whoop Sean. Hell, it's bones, this is half the game! One's got to talk slick!

Suddenly, the cell block door opened. When a screw or jailer entered, they made so much noise no one could miss it. This is just the way the system is set up; when the controllers come, there is no surprise. This is a little contrary to what is taught in society.

Thay got up to look out of their cell. "Dewayne?" He watched him park a cart with all his belongings in front of the cell.

"They're moving trustees out to put them back here. I told them I would go into this cell. The last cell is gonna be filled with three more brothers. The other block that is down from here will be filled with trustees, too. This place is crazy overloaded!"

Sean was sitting at the steel table listening, "That sucks." He got up to help Dewayne put his stuff into the cell. He noticed he had a mattress, "there are only two bunks? Where are you gonna sleep?"

"The floor," Dewayne replied. He pulled a long plastic portable bed into the cell. In jail they called them a boat.

They both helped Dewayne get his stuff into the cell. They cleaned the area where the boat was going to be placed. In the joint, or jail, a boat is a plastic tub that lays on the floor for a man to sleep. It raises him above the cold concrete floor. Once Thay had it cleaned, Sean squatted down to place it where Dewayne wanted it. He saw Dewayne wipe it again so he helped. As he duck squatted, Dewayne kept looking at him.

"What? I'm trying to help. You want it cleaner; that's cool. I'm just trying to help!"

"Sorry, I was just looking at you," Dewayne smiled. "I'm not trying to make you mad. I was just looking. You know, your meat in your boxers is showing. You're squatting down, your boxers are tight right now. That big thing is running down your leg!" Dewayne giggled, "it looks nice! Like a long log with two walnuts."

"Oh!" Sean was so use to his long swipe and large nuts he did not think about it! "You like my meat? It is like an elephant trunk! You a size queen?" He laughed with Dewayne. "Sorry, didn't mean to get on you."

"No, I'm not. You might make me into one, though! I know you didn't mean to get on me. I'm sorry about looking, but you do things sometimes without realizing it. Like, …and I'm trying to be smooth…you act like your penis is the same as everyone else's. It sure is long!" Dewayne smiled. "You got a long one! I am just saying. You know Thay and I like dick. You got a long dick. I got to look." As they cleaned, Dewayne noticed Sean's penis somewhat swelled. Once done, he watched Sean stand in front of him. He pulled on his boxers to loosen and adjust them.

He watched Sean do his thing without realizing it. His pipe swelled to semi-hard. In the boxers, his penis print pushed on the material. He was not erect by no means, but when Sean heard that kind complement the blood flowed through his swipe. He felt good that he was around two men that understood.

Dewayne asked, "yo, y-all wants some party favorites?"

Sean watched Dewayne take a drip from a little bottle to put it on his tongue. "What's that?"

Thay responded, "something that will make you feel good."

Again, Dewayne said, "do you want to try some?" Dewayne was a smooth brother like Thay.

Yet, Sean did not know Dewayne. Thay and Dewayne were cool because they knew each other from the streets. Sean was lucky that he was with them: gay and all. However, trust is something that is built.

Dewayne was a dark-skinned brother with five inches of soft meat. He had more body hair, too. He was slim with little muscular build. However, he still looked good.

"Okay. What is it?"

Thay replied, "ecstasy."

"I think I had this before."

Dewayne gave Sean directions. He told Sean to lean his head back to stick out his tongue. When he lifted the little bottle, Sean should bring his tongue up then lean back. Sean complied, but Dewayne gently grabbed his mohawk pulling his head back further. Dewayne gave him a little extra. When he was done, he said, "I just wanted to make sure you did it right." He rubbed his fingers on Sean's stomach.

Sean loved that he pulled his hair and softly touched his stomach. When he did this to him, he naturally slid his hand into his boxer to massage his swipe. Shit like this made Sean horny. "That shit has a funky taste," he noted. He watched both Thay and Dewayne smile, then they started cleaning more. Sean pulled down more on his boxers. He didn't know it, but his trimmed man hairs above his swipe were showing. The top of his swipe held up his boxers.

Inside his boxers, the end of his swipe head was sliding out of its hood. He felt good being with them. Yet, sometimes he was embarrassed about his swipe swelling around them.

As Sean cleaned, his swipe swelled to eleven inches. His brain keep repeating to him the sensation of Dewayne feeling his stomach. He could feel his penis head touching the material of the boxers. A man's swipe swells a little; it is gonna happen. This is why he pulled his boxers down as low as he could. Hell, he was glad Dewayne had all those cleaning supplies and got him high.

He noticed when they were in the cell alone both of them would act more feminine. More tender. You know, more outward with him and themselves. He got hornier being around them. It was a small narrow cell. If they were not looking, he would stroke his swipe, then push it more downward in his shorts. All this moving around allowed it to sometimes show more on his boxers.

When they cleaned, Thay and Dewayne both would bump into him now and then, or touch his waist or the top of his ass. Sometimes, they would act like they accidentally bumped his swipe. The more they were around him doing this, the more his gaydar would send pleasurable sensations through his brain and swipe. The ecstasy had him so focused on the moment.

When Thay took a moment from cleaning, he adjusted Sean's boxers for him so they were a little off-center. This let his swipe run clearly into the one side of the leg area. Thay and Dewayne could see the drugs had made him horny. Were they turning him out? Or, was Sean turning them out?

Sean started to feel like the great elephant with a long, heavy trunk around two bitches which needed to be mated. He stretched out to twelve inches. He was ready to mate. He was not sure what to say, but he had to say something. "I wish I had my red strap on because my swipe keeps rubbing on my leg."

Sean watched them strip to their boxers. Thay's meat was hard. It was poking straight out. Dewayne's meat was half hard. They didn't pull on their meat like Sean would now and then. They just kept doing their thing: cleaning and all.

Thay would sometimes bend over next to him. Since his boxer were lose, they would slide off his ass. Occasionally, he turned away from Sean backing his ass into his upper leg. Other times, he would squeeze his body past Sean as he was cleaning the upper part of the wall.

When he did, he would bump against his swipe. A few times he flat out touched it with his fingertips to feel its thickness, then would say, *"oops, excuse me."*

Dewayne was doing the same type stuff with Sean. Dewayne would ask him now and then to help him clean the bottom of the wall. Sean would pull his boxer's leg up as he squatted. It would tighten around his swipe, forcing it to slide a little out the leg. It was all wet and creamy. Sometimes it pulsated. Various times when Dewayne rose to stand, he put a hand on Sean's upper leg next to his swipe.

Other times, Dewayne and Thay stood together. Dewayne complained his lower back hurt from the bending. Thay would pull down the back of his underwear to rub it. Other moments, Dewayne would look at Thay's swollen penis, commenting, *"really Thay? Really? You got to play with your booty more often."*

When Sean watched, he naturally stroked his pipe.

* * *

Like Dewayne said, the jailers brought in the other three brothers. Thay told Sean not to face them because of his meat.

"Okay," Sean replied. At this point, his high was flying through him; it felt so good. Once the jailers were done, they put them on lockdown letting them all know at 6:00 am they would be out. By this time, all three of their swipes retracted to a more normal state. Supper would come at 5:00 pm. The doors slammed and they were gone.

Once they left, Dewayne went to stand in the shower. He lite a joint. Thay saw it so he stepped into the small one-man shower stall. Thay was massaging Dewayne's swipe as he took a pull. "It will make your high feel more intense if I play with you."

"Sean," Dewayne said, "you want some? We both are friends, you can be too."

"Sure, that ecstasy is great. My mind is so focused." His swipe was again pressed hard on his boxers bouncing around like any man's partial erection. "Now, I see why you bitches started cleaning so hard. Like, I can focus my mind on every dirt spot!" He laughed, then he noticed he got some looks from Thay and Dewayne. "What?"

Dewayne cracked on him first, "Oh, we're bitches now. You the big swipe of the house?" Dewayne watched Sean stretch to step on the opening ledge of the shower to exhale toward the shower vent, his swipe print forced his boxer out further. Dewayne grabbed it, "I bet you would like this bitch to touch this meat!" He pulled it out so they all could look at it.

Sean passed the joint to Thay, then removed his boxers. "Yeah, I would. Am I the big brother in the house who has to mate with you." He laughed, high, "like in the old days when they would put the big brother with a bitch to fuck. You gonna take advantage of me and force me to sex you up!" He laugh, again. "I'm cool with that!"

Thay took a hit. Then, Thay played with Sean's meat. "Sean, you can fit in here, too. If you do that, it will help all the smoke go into the vent." He handed the joint to

Dewayne. Thay helped Sean climb in, he felt his body touch his. Occasionally, his swipe wiggled and hit both of them. Thay would keep looking down to watch. The tip of it all wet and left a spot on his leg. It was so beautiful.

Dewayne started to gently touch Sean. "I see you got an erection started! Like you said, you need to mate."

"Big swipe needs sex, Dewayne," Thay noted.

After Dewayne handed Sean the joint, he commented, "that depends if that swipe can handle two bitches." Dewayne grabbed his nut sack as he stretched to blow smoke into the vent, "think these tight nuts of yours can do all that." He squeezed them watching Sean spread his legs and stand on tiptoes. "You felt that, didn't you?"

Sean moaned, excited, "I like my nuts being squeezed! Shit turns me on, like you two bitches bumping into me while I'm cleaning!" He stroke his meat multiple times, "see, it's all creamy on the end. You didn't think I would notice?"

Suddenly, they heard the door slam at the farthest end of the block. The screw yelled it was supper time. Sean reached for his boxer to put them on as fast as he could. When he did, he noticed Dewayne watching his swipe fall out of the fly as he pulled them up. Sean's swipe was fully swollen to thirteen inches. He forced it into the boxers. When Dewayne stepped out of the shower stall, he told Sean to sit at the table.

He was helping Sean. He said he would get his tray. Sean was high, but he figured it out. His swipe was hard as hell lying on his leg. If he moved, he felt the warm hardness. He knew if the screw saw, it would bring on suspicion.

Thay helped too, "here; be fast," he quickly pushed Sean's swipe down between his legs, "sit up straighter and arch your back in to hide that meat!" He quietly whispered, "we don't want them to see you hard-n-all. They may come back to search."

"Grab the trays," the screw said.

They sat eating their meal. Every now and then, both Dewayne and Thay looked over at Sean's meat. They both loved its length. The swelling dropped with the interruption. Yet, it no way retracted all the way.

* * *

Eventually, Sean interrupted their sexual fantasies, "I got to get a hold of my Unck." Sean noted, "I got to get some money sent up here." He stood up for a second to shake his swipe into the leg area of his boxers.

Thay got up with him to roll his elastic on his boxers. "They'll ride a little higher, but your swipe won't keep opening your fly."

"Yeah, now my swipe is running more down my leg! You like that, don't you? See a brotha's swipe pressing outward! I got to shower to wash it off."

Thay giggled like a hoe, "yeah. You look good like an elephant."

Dewayne switched the subject, "you can't reach your uncle?"

"No. The phone system only allows me to call every thirty minutes. He ain't recognizing the number so he doesn't take the call. If I could only call his phone three time, then send a text to let him know it was me. I know he would call back." Now that they were talking about daily life, Sean's swipe lost its blood. His horniness left for a few.

"That is strange," Dewayne noted. "That is like some kind of G-14 classified."

"You don't know my Unck. If I do that, he will call. Sorry, that is my life. It is what it is."

"I got a cell phone. I hope you're serious."

Sean replied, "like a heart attack. If I connect with him, I'll be cool. I need some funds. Please?"

"Well, don't burn up the battery up, I need it, too. I can't get to a place all the time to charge it." Dewayne dug through his items, then laid the phone on the table. "I'm trusting you. You better be straight!"

Sean grabbed it doing exactly what he said. He sat the phone on the table, "he'll call in a minute. You all cool with me, I want to get some funds to help pay my way. I don't want two brothers kicking me in my nuts! Especially two brother that need swipe!" He joked. He felt Thay reach over and pull on the leg of his boxers so his swipe head was exposed. He took his index finger and very gently massaged its wetness.

"Can you get cash?" Dewayne asked.

"How much?"

"Five twenties? Maybe ten?"

"I'll ask for ten Grants; fifties!" Sean noticed both of their surprise. "You don't know my Unck." He chuckled. The phone lit up. "Hello. Unck? I'm in county using someone else's cell phone. I need help, but I can't talk too long." Sean explained what he needed. "Okay, Unck, I know I fucked up, but I can't burn up this phone. I know you have been there for me!" He paused. "Yes, one did mention that to me. I don't know how to connect," he paused again, "okay, if I see him I will talk to him. Okay, bye." He placed it on the table.

* * *

Thay, Dewayne, and Sean went through a moment. Sean felt bad about his uncle. He appreciated them. Then, they took time to clean more, suck and fuck, then go to bed. Sean did them, but not like he wanted too! This day was like foreplay sex! Thay and Dewayne were now more comfortable around him. Sean didn't know it, but they both wanted more action, too!

7. Gettin Lucky in County

Sean was concerned about what his uncle told him. He had a hard time sleeping. He knew he would come through, he just did not know how.

* * *

The next morning, the jailer came through. "Dewayne? You ready to go to work, Dewayne?"

Dewayne replied, "yes sir." As he moved from leaning on the wall by the door, he felt his booty. It was a little sore! He liked Sean, he made him feel good.

"Which one of you is Sean Jones?"

Sean peeked out of his sheet, "me." It was the jailer who mentioned his uncle's name.

"Get up, you have an attorney visit."

"At this time?"

"Yes, they said she drove up from Chicago. She wants to see you…N-O-W! Get dressed and let's go!"

"Oh, shit. It's lawyer Ryan." He got up with a morning hard-on in his boxers. "Lawyer Ryan don't play." He got dressed as fast as he could; cuffed, and walked out.

Sean made it back about 10:00 am. Thay noticed he sure was there for a while. They sat and made small talk.

Sean told Thay he was now straight and had some money on his account. "I'm sure happy about that."

Dewayne and the other trustees were brought back for lunch. They usually came back about this time to sit around until noontime or after. They would all get locked in while the screws did a count throughout the whole jail. Since it was so overcrowded, it now took longer.

* * *

"How'd your lawyer visit go, Sean?" Dewayne asked. "Good. I got your shit, too."

"What? On a lawyer visit."

"I told you, you don't know my Unck. Don't ask!"

"You seem upset?"

"No, got stuff on my mind."

After the meal, Sean pulled off his boxers to get on the toilet. Both Thay and Dewayne watch his six-inch soft swipe bounce around while it hung off his tight nuts. He tossed a bunch of toilet paper in the bowel to squeeze out two balloons. "Can y'all look away!"

Thay and Dewayne politely looked the other way when he forced them out. Sean took care of his business. "Here, $100 ought to get you started," he gave Dewayne two fifties. "Promise me you're not that dumb to let them other three with us know anything about this."

"Don't worry, I do everything G-14 classified. They don't know I fuck around! Thay and you are the only people that know. Also, the jailer I get it from; he is a family

112

member." Dewayne finished, "that must be one hell of a lawyer you got!"

"Family lawyer. Like I said, you don't know my Unck, don't ask me anymore about it."

"G-14 classified!" Dewayne chuckled.

"G-14 classified!"

* * *

The screw opened the block door, then walked the alleyway in front of the cellblock, "count!" As the screw passed, he informed them, "you'll be probably on lockdown until tomorrow, we're having trouble in another part of the jail." It was the jailer Sean knew.

Thay commented, "that sucks."

"Great," Dewayne said.

As the jailer walked away, Sean noted, "I see you two already hittin the ecstasy."

"You want some?" Dewayne asked, "we might as well get high and watch TV."

"Damn, that was a big amount, like three or four drops!"

Dewayne put his hand on Sean's upper leg, then whispered, "we're good, I'll get more now I got cash." After a little time, he noticed again that Sean was getting horny. When he took the ecstasy, his swipe would grow a little hard. "Sean, I got them pills…"

"What pills?" Sean interrupted.

"Them pills that make your swipe hard!" He teased. "The big swipe of the house might like them! I want some more action!"

They both glanced at his boxers.

"It is half hard now, I want to pull it!" Sean chuckled. "My swipe stays hard!" He stood in front of them to pull his boxers down. When he did this, he stroked it. He pulled his shorts up.

"These will help so Thay and I can milkjizzle you!" Dewayne noted as he pushed his booty outward, put a hand on his hip, leaned his head back, and batted his eyes.

"Milkjizzle me?" Sean watched Dewayne get ready to give him two. "Okay. Why two?"

"So, we can milkjizzle the big swizzle in the house." Thay giggled. "We're gonna be locked in 'till morning. We're all rested, the cell is clean, what else is there to do?"

"So, you want to turn me out!" Sean laughed. He sat on the steel table seat, but it was cold. Sean got up to get a folded sheet, both Thay and Dewayne watched his swipe bounce around. When Sean was getting the sheet ready, it stuck out his boxer's fly. It was hard as hell! He started pulling on it, "I need to jag!"

As Sean prepared his area to sit, his erection would fade then fill again. Thay helped him. With Thay gently touching his body, it would only fade to ten inches. Thay was again walking around with a full erection. Sean stared at it, lusting.

Sean sat it on the steel seat, then pulled off everything, but his socks. He casually sat to face Thay and Dewayne. He watched them both stare. This made him hornier. They liked looking at him. He eventually got up to stand in front of the toilet to get all his piss out. It took a moment with a hard swipe. He turned so they could watch him flick his swipe a few times!

He sat back down, sitting very straight. He pushed his swipe between his legs because he loved the pressure feeling it created. Sometimes, he brought his legs apart, "Fucking place, it is hot. You right, Dewayne, those pills work! Fuck, my swipe won't go down." He sat in front of them jagging it. "I'm gonna knock one out in front of the two of you. Watch me cream!"

Thay and Dewayne watched him stop jerking to force it down between his legs. They could see the way he sat, his nuts and swipe showed hanging below his legs. If he opened his legs, his nuts pushed his swipe higher and it would bounce up sometimes to his belly. There was a couple of time when his swipe hit his belly, precum flew off leaving a wet spot. They both loved his show. He was loving the way they were looking at him.

Sean smiled, high as hell, "what's up? I want some more today, we got all this time on our hands!" He laughed again. "What you looking at?"

Dewayne was smiling ear to ear, "I'm just looking at your smooth, cut body, and that meat hanging between your legs. You are hiding it? You sitting with your legs tight. Open them again so I can see a tight nut brother!"

Both Dewayne and Thay could not stop watching him.

Sean laughed, high, "it feels great. If I rock, my nuts to rub on that bed sheet. The pressure feels great." He started to gently wiggle again, then pushed his swipe and nuts between his legs harder. "Man, my nuts love it!"

Thay gently put his fingers tips on Sean's shoulder, then slid them down his chest. He took his hand away. Dewayne bumped the back of his hand on Sean's nipple.

"You two keep touching my body and acting so sexual around me."

Thay giggled, "yeah! You're dripping jism!"

Thay grabbed a folded blanket to sit on the floor next to Sean. He stripped naked, standing in front of Sean with a hard swipe. "Here, I'll help." He reached under his legs, playing with a swipe and nut sack. He first ran a finger over his swipe head to collect its juices then licked it.

Sean's body wanted to ejaculate more when he saw this.

"I guess we're stuck in this cell for a while." Dewayne joked, as he got naked, too. "Like you said, you need some." He observe Sean lean forward, he looked like he was sitting on the toilet. This helped his swipe hang lower. Dewayne started to gently touch Sean's nipples with a fingertip.

Sean felt Thay pull on his nuts harder. He worked his swipe faster! Sean sat up straight and opened his legs. "O-o-h!" Sean gasped.

"Maybe we should take Sean to the bunk, Dewayne," Thay suggested. When it got totally hard, his foreskin pulled back. It let his lighter colored head show so beautifully!

"Get on the bunk and hold your knees to your chest," Dewayne commented.

Sean got up to try it. He laid on his side holding his knees with his arm. He arched his back little. Dewayne and Thay climbed on the bunk. Sean felt Thay get busy again. Now, Thay could run his fingers over his booty, too. Thay's thumb was rubbing on his booty hole while his fingers pulled his nuts. He felt Dewayne rubbing his body and kissing his lips. Sometimes Dewayne would so softly play with his swipe head, too.

"All that touching feels great," Sean whispered. "I love foreplay…. O-o-h…"

"I will give you a milking from behind." Thay got Dewayne to sit in front of Sean.

Sean saw Dewayne's hard penis, "I like your meat."

Thay instructed Sean to lay doggy style with his shoulder on Dewayne's lap. Thay knelt behind him using both hands on his swipe, "how's that working?" He kept pulling and stroking. He licked in his booty hole now and then. He felt Sean wiggle. When he did it, Thay pulled on his nuts harder until he stopped moving!

Sean moaned, "you two are turning me out! I'm in old master's house where I have to sleep with two bitches. I have to put my seed into you both."

Thay said, laughing, "yeah, get off! Let me work the big swipe of the house!"

Sean laid with his head and shoulders into Dewayne's lap. He felt his warmth. "Do me!" He started licking on Dewayne's pipe. He watched it bounce around!

Thay pulled on Sean's swipe and massaged his booty hole. His tongue licked his crack. "How's that? Want me to pull harder on these nuts!"

Sean moaned, "O-o-h, milk me!" He was now sucking Dewayne's swipe. His brain hit its pleasure zone, all this touching on him; he loved it. "Pull my nuts harder, Thay!" He was excited for rougher sex. He had to stop for those few precious seconds holding Dewayne swipe in his mouth.

Both Dewayne and Thay watched him. His body started to uncontrollably spasm, his orgasm came. Dewayne rubbed his upper back more. Sean felt Dewayne's finger reach down to his crack area so he arched his back as much as he could. Thay grabbed a towel to throw it between his legs. He rubbed the end of his swipe with his palm as he was cumming. This increased the pleasure of it all! All his cum made it supper-slippery which sent so much pleasure through his brain.

"Suck on me, Big Swipe," Dewayne planted both hands on his head. Sean felt Dewayne get ready to bust. Sean moaned as he felt Thay start to suck on him. He lite up Dewayne's swipe as he felt him cum into his mouth. Dewayne was cut with a smaller swipe head. Sean could roll his tongue around it and take it all in as he did his blowjizzle.

Who was really the innocent one?

Dewayne was quietly moaning, "a-w-w…" He felt cum rocket out his penis into Sean's mouth. "Taste it all."

When Sean finished, he looked at his swipe, "damn, it didn't even drop. It is so sensitive after cumming." He started again to finish Dewayne's blowjizzle. He wanted all his cum!

As he did this, Dewayne put his legs up on the bottom of the bunk. "Get some of that while I'm laying here, Big Swipe. I'll be your bitch." Dewayne pulled his booty open with his hands.

This excited Sean, his meat got heavy again.

Thay greased Dewayne's hole, Sean's swipe, and tucked a pillow under Dewayne's lower back. "Easy, Thay," he jerked a little as Thay applied the grease, "it's sensitive!" Sean slid his swipe very slowly into Dwayne.

At first, he could barely take the sensitivity, but the pleasure of it started to grow. His brain started to send more hormones through his body. "I can barely do this, but it feels so good," he moaned as he fucked Dewayne a little faster. The sensitivity was masked by his brain entering its pleasure zone. His swipe bounced out a few times, but Dewayne quickly guided it back in.

It took about fifteen minutes this time. Sean felt his body uncontrollably jerk. "I'm getting there."

"Do me, Big Swipe…Take that ass…"

Sean kept tapping that sh-zit until he blew again! He was pumping on Dewayne's ass as hard as he could. He had his arms next to his side with his legs fully extended lifting himself on his toes. It looked like he was doing push-ups, but instead he was thrusting his waist to pound his swipe into him. The pounding caused Dewayne to start to slide off the bunk! "A-w-e…, a-w-e…, where you going, boo-boo, give me that shit!"

Thay watched as he rubbed Sean's body. "Keep fucking him."

Dewayne moaned, "fuck me, Big Swipe! I'm not going anywhere." He grabbed the iron bed posts.

Thay loved watching him pound his swipe into Dewayne! Eventually, Thay knelt on the bunk by Dewayne's head to help keep him from sliding off. He started rubbing Dewayne's chest and leaning on him. "Come on, Big Swipe, take that shit."

"Fuck," Sean moaned, "I got this! You bitches gonna get fuck now you gave me all the sh-zit! I will hit you both, twice. Thay you're next." He rocked into Dewayne deep! He knew Dewayne could feel all thirteen inches. "What bitch? This meat too big for you to take." Sean pounded harder, "you wanted some dick, now you can't handle this?" He started kissing on Thay.

"No, Big Swipe," Dewayne moaned, "A-w-e...o-o-h..."

"I'm the big swipe of the house." Sean looked at Dewayne's pleasure.

"Okay, Big Swipe." Dewayne gasped quietly. "Do me like a hoe!" He moaned some more. "Do me..."

"What, bitch?" He tapped Dewayne faster.

"You the big swipe of the house." Dewayne moaned in more pleasure, "take that shit, Big Swipe. Guerrilla fuck me. Make me feel it!"

That turned on Sean. Thay was rubbing both their bodies. Sean watched Dewayne let his head lay between Thay's legs. "Stay on my swipe, bitch!" Sean told Thay to put his swipe in Dewayne mouth and move closer. "O-o-h," he bit Thay's neck gently, "I am cumming...! Take this sh-zit, bitch."

"Okay," Dewayne murmured, "fuck me! You Big Swipe! Do it! Cum in me. Mate me!" Dewayne went back to suck Thay's dick.

Sean rode him a little longer then slowed down. He slowly pulled out, his swipe maybe dropped an inch! His nut sack barely loosened. He released Dewayne and got up to wipe his swipe with a wet washcloth. Then he came to the front of the bunk where he knelt a little in front of Dewayne, "lick on this swipe head. Get it hard again for Thay."

Thay instantly climbed onto the bunk to swallow Dewayne's swipe. You could hear Thay slobbering over it. "I got you, Dewayne!" Thay felt Sean put his hands on his booty.

Sean watched Thay work on Dewayne. He was pulling his nut, bouncing his head up and down. Dewayne's legs twitched, his muscle spasms started again. He grabbed Sean's legs with his hands. "O-h…"

"I see you are pro pole greaser, too!" Sean said to Thay.

When Dewayne unloaded, Thay swallowed it all. "O-o-h; Fuck!"

* * *

They all took a moment to get into the shower to smoke a quick joint and take some more ecstasy. Sean's swipe hung hard. They both gently played with it. They noticed that Sean would get very excited if his swipe was gently touched with finger tips.

This got Sean going again. Thay's swipe was pointing upward, hard. He grabbed Thay. "Get down and open your legs! I'm gonna do you." He watched Thay comply. Sean bent over, but he was too tall with the bunk above him. He wanted a better position.

He picked up Thay. He felt Thay's booty crack on his swipe as he carried him to the steel table where a blanket covered most of the top. He laid Thay down, pushed apart his legs, and put one foot on the metal table seat. Suddenly, he felt Dewayne grab his nuts from behind! "You like that nut sack, too? Pull and squeeze it while I do your friend!"

Dewayne replied, "Do him. Put it in him slowly! Thay got that tight hole!" As he held Sean's nuts, passionately lusting, "let me get you nice and excited again!" Dewayne kissed him on the back making sure he rubbed his forearm on Sean's booty crack.

Sean moaned as he looked at Thay. Dewayne's nut sack massage got him back on point.

He could feel his arm hairs on his booty so he spread his leg open as far as he could. When he looked down at Thay, he saw he was naturally cumming with a swipe inside of him. He saw his body occasionally contract. He felt his booty hole tighten then loosen. "A-w-e," his muscles were already twitching. He could not control himself as he ran his swipe in and out of Thay. He pounded him harder to get off. "Man, you got a booty hole! That shit is on fire right now. I will loosen it up."

"Do me, Big Swipe, take that shit!" Thay moaned. He wanted Sean to do him hard, he was gone in his pleasure zone. It was a new experience for him to have something that long go in and out that fast.

Sean bent down more and locked onto Thay so he couldn't slide away. "I got you, your booty will loosen with me in it." Sean whispered, breathing heavily now into his ear. "Aww…a-w-w…" Sean naturally opened his mouth to bite his neck. It took some time, but he busted again!

Dewayne rubbed Sean's body as he cummed, whispering, "get off, Big Swipe, you run the cell. You the big swipe, run that swipe into that hole!"

Sean felt Dewayne rub his hands over his booty crack, then his nuts. Sean moaned, "y-e-a-h," he bit Thay in the neck harder! "Boo-Boo's gonna respect this fucking," he whispered.

Thay lay there moaning, "stretch that that sh-zits, get it opened up for you." As Thay felt Sean cum, he felt every muscle spasm in Sean's jaw, "bite me like a bitch, keep me on that swipe." He rolled his head a little to the side. "Take that sh-zit like you can fuck!"

* * *

It was a long night in the cell. When the door slammed that the screws used, Thay and Dewayne told him to sit with his back toward them. Sean was getting ready to tap them again, hanging with them and sensing their actions, it kept making him horny. When he sat, his penis print showed clearly in his boxers. It held the leg area open.

Thay sat down slowly, "my booty hole is getting sore!"

"Good," Sean quietly replied, as the jailer walked the runway, "'cause I'm gonna hit your tight hole again. Break it in better! Open up your tight spot."

Thay smiled, "you're so horny…"

Sean interrupted, "Always!"

"Damn," Dewayne teased, "you fucked us both twice already. This is gonna take a while, let's do some more party favorites!"

While they stood in the little shower area, both Dewayne and Thay would feel Sean's body. They now acted differently around Sean. They did not touch his swipe, but they would give him friendly gestures. Dewayne would occasionally run a hand on his booty crack, hold his waist, make a few polite sexual comments, kiss him, and put a hand on his chest massaging his nipples. Thay liked his six pack on his stomach so he occasionally ran his finger tips over it, then bring them down to play with the little patch of hair he left above his swipe. Sometimes, he went further to move his hand down next to his nut sack, and feel the side of his booty. He knelt somewhat. Sean's swipe wiggled around on his forearm.

* * *

After they were done the third time, they all were worn out. Sean lay on the bunk on his side, "get over here, Thay." His swipe dripped onto the blanket. He lift one knee for comfort.

Thay came over to the bunk, then he greased Sean's swipe again. He climbed on the bunk to push Sean slowly into his hole. "A-w-e," he repeated as Sean started to slowly running his snake into him. "A-w-e...O-o-h-h-h-h-h..." This time Sean's swipe did not reach the point of no return. Sean laid it into him to make him feel good.

* * *

As you can see Sean knew the nuances of county jail life. Depending on the jail, the prisoner underground operated at various levels. His boring days were eased by his two friends.

8. Trouble Comes in County

The days in county were going good for Sean and his two new friends. Sean took a liking for Thay. He liked his tight ass, but he liked him as a person, too. Thay's gaydar reacted toward Sean, it was like he knew Sean and him had a good thing. Thay shared it with Dewayne and they agreed that Thay should think about it. He was glad he had two new gay friends and hoped after the stay in county he could still hang with them.

* * *

Yet, the day happened. It was a day that no man wants to come. Sean, Thay, Dewayne, and two of the three other trustees were in the cellblock. Thay hit the shower in the block instead of the shower in their cell. The block showers worked better. One of the other trustees saw him go into the shower so he joined him. Thay was showering in a stall that Sean and Dewayne could see him. They would all keep an eye on each other when out in the bullpen with the rest of the prisoners. Suddenly, Thay was out of sight and they heard loud noises from the shower. It sounded like a fight.

Sean started to get up, but Dewayne grabbed his hand. "You can't do this because they have a camera in here. I know the blind spots, this is an old unit. I got this, but you have to work with me. Thay will make it. We can save him. Plus, the other trustee is leaving. They'll be here next. He is standing by the exit door."

Sean's heart tore. He could only focus on the shower area. It was burning inside him.

Dewayne quickly got up to head for the cell. He walk quickly to the block door, the jailer opened it to shout for the other trustee, but he was already there waiting with Dewayne. The jailer stepped back as the man stepped out so Dewayne slapped wet toilet paper on the lens of the camera. "I need a roll of toilet paper."

As soon as he slammed the door close, Sean jumped into action, "T...H...A...Y!" He had murder on the mind.

Thay crawled out of the entrance with the other man following. "What you gonna do, bitch?" The man shouted.

Sean got him three times in the neck while he was talking. The trustee bum-rushed Sean swinging like a mad man. Most of his blows were haymakers to Sean's stomach or head. He was trying to knock the wind out of Sean. He felt the bulldozer method would work.

What the man did not know about Sean was that he would kill and was well-trained in fighting. The haymakers to his guts were nothing to Sean. On the last haymaker, Sean got him with a hard jab to the throat, "deep throat that, BITCH! I'LL KILL YOU!"

The man staggered back, coughing. "Fuck you."

"Where you going, BITCH?" Sean moved in with three more quick jabs, they were all to his nut sack. Once the man hit his knees and leaned on one hand, Sean put him into a sleeper hold, "goodnight, B-I-A-T-C-H! You may never wake up!"

Thay ran to their cell. He sat on the lower bunk. He pulled a sheet over his naked body and held his legs tight with his arms. All he could think about was how the man had tried to put his swipe into him. He cried.

* * *

Dwayne instantly warned Sean they had to hurry, the jailer would be back with one trustee and do a round for count. "We have to clean this up!"

"Okay." Sean dragged the man back into the shower where the water would miss him. He tossed around bars of soap and put the man's shower shoes out on the floor in the bullpen. He soaped the dude's back and legs, then bounced his head off the wall to give him a lump.

Dewayne was waiting by the door, preparing to remove the toilet paper from the camera. When the exit door opened, "excuse me, sir, I'm on the afternoon schedule for work, should I go now?"

"No, I got to do a round."

They all were in their cell when the guard took a pass. While Sean was dragging the man back into the shower, Dewayne got Thay to lie down. Sean stood brushing his teeth by the sink.

After the guard passed, Dewayne whispered to Sean, "he tried to put that nasty fucking thing between his legs into Thay."

Sean coughed, spitting out toothpaste, "what! In Thay?" Sean's eyes went red.

"Lockdown, lockdown," the screw yelled running passed the bullpen area, *"stay in your cells."* On his radio, he yelled, *"medical emergency!!! We have one down!!!"*

* * *

Times were changing for Sean and his new friends. The next morning, Sean, Dewayne and Thay sat in separate interrogation rooms. They, of course, were put into segregation cells the day before. Thay was not doing too good, but he would not tell what happen. Sean hated what that man did to Lil-Thay. It burned deep in him. He still had murder on the mind.

Sean had two detectives sitting before him who wanted answers. Sean wanted street justice. The detectives said all three were being charged with attempted murder and a bunch of other minor crap. Welcome to America!

"We need you to sign this paper," one detective placed it in front of Sean, "I'll uncuff you to sign."

"Don't bother, I want a lawyer."

The second detective went into his routine with Sean, but he saw Sean ignored it. "You're facing 30 years in this state!"

"I didn't do anything!" Sean fired back.

"Sure!!!"

* * *

There was a knock at the door, then it opened. Lawyer Ryan stepped through the door with me following. "Hello, gentlemen, I'm Rebecca Ryan, Attorney at Law. This is my client."

The guard on Unck's payroll informed them.

One detective fired back, "we don't have any paperwork…"

"I know," she interrupted, placing two pieces of paper in front of Sean, "I'm on record as his attorney. Here are his and the two other men involved, I'm the attorney of record with the court. I want to see them." She impatiently stared at them. "Did you hear what I said? Now, gentlemen!" *The pit-bull had arrived.*

Lawyer Ryan worked her magic. It took about a month, but she had all three of them out of segregation. She got a signed court order which said they all three should be placed in the same cellblock by themselves for protection. How she did that surprised all of us.

* * *

The man who had attacked Thay wanted charges brought against Sean. He was in the hospital. He yelled at the officers and state attorney. Yet, later on he received a visit from his older brother.

"Bro, you got to drop it. Let it go. You made a mistake. When you fell, you bumped your head. It fucked up your memory!"

"I ain't letting anything go! The motherfucker did me!"

"I got a visit from god or the reaper. Me and Mama will be harmed! Feel me? You fucked with the wrong

129

motherfucker! Do you think they are going to stop there? Just shut your mouth!"

* * *

"So, your Honor," Lawyer Ryan was finishing in court, "we heard from the very man who said he was assaulted by this man. Yet, today he can't seem to remember all the facts. I think we have a problem with the state attorney." She turned toward Sean, Thay, and Dewayne.

She looked over them to see Kareem sitting behind the man's brother and mother. She watched Kareem lift his fingers to wave. She turned back to the judge. "Your Honor, at this time I move that all charges be dropped." She stepped behind Sean, putting a hand on his shoulder, "clearly there is no evidence. The camera footage was a waste of time. The investigation was handled haphazardly. I also move for a motion to reduce their time spent in county, set a hearing for bail, and the motion."

"I agree, charges dismissed," the judge replied. "Set a hearing date as soon as possible for the motions before this court!"

"Your Honor," the DA stood, "we have enough evidence to charge and convict."

"Be patient, Sean," Lawyer Ryan whispered, "be patient, gentlemen."

The judge hit his hammer on the bench, "gentlemen, what do you expect? You brought a case to me totally unprepared! I cannot do anything else but dismiss it."

"Thanks, Lawyer Ryan," Sean said, quietly. He glanced at me sitting in the room.

Sean was the first to be placed in a small cellblock in the old section of the jail. He got a supply bag from the jailer. "Awe, sir, could I get extra razors and extra soap? These razors don't work very well." It was the jailer that knew Whitey.

He was in the old medical cell area with a great deal of dust. Sean immediately headed to the shower, he wanted to remove his patchy beard and body hair. He liked his swipe clean-shaven with his little patch of hair. He was in the shower shaving around his tight nut sack and the top of his swipe when he heard the jailer bring someone else in. He did not look. He hurried as fast as he could, yet being careful.

Moments later, Thay poked his head around the shower wall to see who was in it. He did not want any more trouble.

"Thay!" Sean said immediately. His penis got heavy and his head slid out somewhat from its foreskin.

Thay smiled. "I missed you, Sean." Thay quickly walked to the end of the shower cage, around the back wall, then to Sean. There was a camera pointed at the shower entrance. He grabbed Sean, feeling his immediate erection against him. "Hold me, Sean." He felt Sean reach between their bodies to lift his swipe. It swelled to thirteen plus inches. "Big Swipe is horny!" Thay giggled. "I missed you, too. I feel your trunk! Thanks for your help."

"I missed you more than you know, Thay." He hugged him tighter.

"Oh, Sean…"

Sean leaned Thay on the shower wall.

Thay moaned, "we can't yet; we have to get some grease. You know I got a tight booty."

"I want your guts," Sean moaned, "I want to feel this in you." Sean was ready to cum, but he did not want to hurt Thay. He just held him. "I need to get off!"

Thay slowly turned around, "I missed you so much." Thay started jagging. He busted on Sean's swipe, then rubbed it all around Sean's penis and nut sack, "I want my scent on my man so another motherfucker will smell it."

Sean watched Thay start to jag him. Thay grabbed his nuts. He moaned, "harder!" Sean grabbed a bar of soap to get his swipe slippery. "O-o-h," Sean moaned, thrusting his swipe back and forth shooting cum into Thay's hand.

"O-o-h, Big Swipe," Thay jagged in front of him, again. He put his cum on him, again. Sean grabbed Thay, hugging and kissing him.

* * *

Well, the day came, Sean was out, but Thay and Dewayne were not. He gave Thay and Dewayne a number to call. He didn't know it, but Thay expressed to Dewayne he was afraid he would never see Sean again.

Sean was with me, he wanted me to be there the day he got out. It gave us time to talk. He knew I wasn't happy with him, but I was happy he was alright.

Sean had a good talk with his Unck.

9. Released

Finally, Dewayne and Thay had their day come to be released. To get out of the pen is a very big moment for any person no matter how long they had been there. They reached out to Sean who promised them a ride home. It was a happy moment for all three.

* * *

Both Dewayne and Thay came out of the jail to meet Sean. Thay was so excited to see Sean. They walked toward the Escalade where Sean stood. There were other men around and other vehicles.

Dewayne whispered to Thay, "nice ride."

The Escalade was all black. This included the rims. Hell, even the hood ornament and emblems were tinted black! The sunlight glistened off the shine of the hood. It also was stretched. Behind the front doors there was an added panel which gave it length. Yet, it looked so clean that anyone would have thought it was made like this. It sure was a looker.

Thay held Sean. "How's my friend?" Thay asked, quietly. "I was scared you wouldn't come. I was so worried.

You know, men inside always say they will see a person on the outside. Then they never do. I have heard it so many times, but now the one that I love is here. Thank you for not breaking my heart."

Sean tighten his grip. "Thay, I got much love for you. I felt it in there, now we can see how it goes out here. I'm better now that I am with you! I love you; Thay. I want to try to make this work." Sean picked up Thay.

"I'm off the ground, you're holding me so tight; Big Swipe!"

"Thay, call me Sean, okay?" Sean let him down.

"I can do that; call you Sean. Sorry." Thay kept his arm around him. "Who is that with you? The man standing over there?" Thay asked, quietly, "He is sort of dressed like you: boots, khakis and a fedora hat. He is also wearing a button shirt. He looks neater. He a thug, too?"

"In a manner of speaking, he is a thug." Sean smiled. "That is my uncle who was with us in court. That is him and his *trilby* hat!" Sean emphasized "trilby".

Thay whispered, "He sure looks different."

"You don't know Unck." Sean's lips opened, he grabbed Thay again. Both their lips met, Sean's tongue entered Thay's mouth. "I feel you against me. I want to fuck you so bad."

"I feel you, too, Big Swipe; I mean Sean." Thay felt his erection against his leg. Thay grabbed Sean harder to rap his legs around his waist. "I want you! I need you to do me! Make me feel good inside so I can forget about this place. Forget all that happened."

* * *

Another Escalade drove passed to park in the front. Two other Cam-am spyders approached.

I looked back, "Sean, we got to go." I watched Sean give me a brief nod. "Sean, did you hear me?"

"Yes, I did," he replied.

* * *

"Hey, Sean," Dewayne smiled. He gave Sean a hug and kiss. He then stepped toward me; politely, "excuse me sir? You must be his uncle?"

"Yeah." I got Sean's attention again waving my index finger in a circular motion. "Security is here. Wrap it up so we can get." I smiled at Dewayne, "po-po shops give me the creeps. It was nice meeting you again, but we got to go."

Dewayne stepped back to Sean.

I stood there, lighting up a cigarette. My brain kept repeating, we got to go! "Gentleman, where to?" I asked with one hand on the Escalade. I could tell Sean was fucking them both, but I had to trust his decisions. This was my family!

"Your uncle is getting a little impatient," Dewayne noted.

"Thay, Dewayne, dhis my Unck." Sean smiled. "In county, y'all never really got a chance to meet. Come on." Sean walked with them both up by Kay and I. "This is Momma Kay. This is Unck. Unck, dhis is Thay. I kind of got a thing with him. And, dhis man is Dewayne. He's cool, too. As you see, he had no problems approaching you."

"Yeah; well, I'm pleased to meet you both. This is Kay." I smiled. "So, what is the plan, Sean? We're in front of the po-po shop. I don't like the po-po shop. You know the deal."

"Hello, gentlemen," Kay replied, "bet you two are glad to be out."

Sean pulled me to the side. "I need a car, can I use this one?" Sean asked, quietly.

"No, this is Momma Kay's car. She needs it to get around in."

Kay excused herself to walk toward the other Escalade. When she did, another man jumped out to stand near Sean and his uncle.

Thay and Dewayne looked at Sean's pants. His meat was pushing out. He kissed Thay, again. Thay's meat was poking out; Dewayne's too.

"Who is that with your Unck?" Dewayne asked.

"That is Tone," Sean whispered.

They watched as Tone approached Sean's uncle. "I got to be sure you are armed, sir. You are the one. Mama Kay will say something if I don't check."

They watched him give Sean's uncle a brief hug feeling for weapons. Then, he walked up to Sean. He put his hands under Sean's arms and felt his chest, "You are not armed, sir?"

"No. Unck has mine."

Tone replied, "We will discuss this later without company."

When the breeze blew lightly, Tone's hoodie opened slightly exposing guns. Thay and Dewayne were surprised. Dewayne whispered to Thay, "did you see what I saw?"

"Sir, it is protocol. Brothers got to be strapped all the time." Tone took one of his guns to park it into Sean's pants; then gave Sean another hug. "You cool?"

"You right, Tone; Mama Kay will say something. I'm good."

Sean looked at Thay and Dewayne as Tone walked away. Sean was horny as hell now. It brought up many good memories. He rubbed his meat.

Tone stood watching the street. He turned toward Sean's uncle. "Sir, we're by po-po. We should go."

Thay and Dewayne were amazed at what just happened; with Tone and all. Big tough Sean had a babysitter! It was like Tone stood near just to case the whole area. "Maybe your uncle is right, Sean, maybe we should move faster," Dewayne replied.

* * *

"So, what is the plan, kid?" They turned as they heard his uncle ask again.

"Hanging out with them for a short moment. Unck, I got to get busy!" He slightly smiled.

"I really need you at work. This is a family business, you got to do what you do. Just remember family first. This is the family business."

"I know, maybe a week, or...? Then, we'll go from there."

"Okay, take the other Escalade, you know Kay uses this one. She'll break my balls if I give it to you." I grabbed my phone, "ya, we're switching cars, okay. Sean wants to use that one." I paused listening. "Okay." Once I hung up, I looked at Tone, "you can go with Sean."

"Yes, sir." He smiled at Sean, Dewayne and Thay. Sean's uncle did not see this. He gave Dewayne a slight nuance of gesture which Sean and Thay picked up.

"See something you like?" Dewayne asked.

"I don't know, yet."

Thay and Dwayne watched two brothers climb out of the first car. "Who are they, Sean." Thay asked, quietly.

"Get me a minute, I got to do this." Sean walked to the group.

"This is getting interesting," Dewayne commented. "They all look like thugs except for Mama Kay. There is something to this." They both stood by the other car watching the group meeting. "Thay, your penis is poking out. Thay, really?"

Thay whispered, "I like him, I can't help it." He giggled.

Tone stepped back, he gestured to Dewayne and Thay, "ready to go?"

As they walked past the group, Sean got their attention, "Thay, Dewayne, this is G-dawg, he is like another uncle. He is Kareem." They had a quick meet and greet.

"Unck, Tone is gonna drive for us. Okay?"

I glanced at Kay, "Sure, it is okay. Stay with them, Tone. Check in with security."

"Yes, Miss Kay."

"Okay people, time to ride," I replied.

* * *

Kareem sat in the front passenger seat, jesting, "All that talk of 'Unck' is making me feel old."

"Shit, you are getting old." G-dawg was driving. He looked the rear mirror at me. "Whitey, do you think the kid will be okay?"

"He is with Tone. You can see he has a liking for the one. He is a grown man, G; we will see. Drop by if you think it is necessary…"

Kareem interrupted, "And, if he ain't, G-dawg, we do a snatch and grab to get him out!"

Mama Kay spoke, "okay you three; we do not know that yet."

"Does Kal know?" I looked at Kay.

"That is their business, Whitey."

"Well, I hoped for a better exit out of county," I noted, "I was at least hoping we all could go to eat or something. All he wants to do is fuck!"

Kareem and G-dawg chuckled.

* * *

Sean was now with his friends who he was waiting on. His parents were concerned with his choices. Whitey was concerned with Sean's relationship with Kal. Yet, he believed in his heart he had found the right one. Who really knows?

10. Thay and Sean

Sean, Thay and Dewayne were finally reunited and alone. They had a great deal of catching up to do. Hopefully, Sean and his friends would become closer. For Sean, it was now a time for wild celebration.

* * *

Thay watched Sean sitting on the kitchen chair, his swipe was pushing on his zipper. He was going to make some quick sandwiches. It slid into his pant leg. He stroked it watching Thay. Thay smiled, "here is a bottle of water." Thay embraced him. "I never want this to end. I missed you so much. I am so horny right now. Do you need some sex?" Thay smiled, sitting on his lap to grind on him. "I want you to feel good, too."

"Hold me," Sean said as he stood.

Thay wrapped his arms tightly around his neck and rapped his legs around his waist. He felt Sean's warm body. "What you doing, Baby?" Thay whispered. He could feel Sean's hand under his booty. He saw Sean's khakis hit the floor. His penis was pushing against his underwear. Thay released him to stand back. "I want to look at your body."

He held both Sean's hands, "I like your red shorts. They are very sexy. You fill them so well."

Thay noticed his shorts were not too tight, nor too lose. They just came to the top of his swipe. He was in bikini style. He could see some of his shaven man hairs because they dipped low in front. They climbed up the sides of his legs to cover his ass just enough.

The bottom of them cupped his large nuts and meat. Their elastic trim ran around Sean's groin so his swipe looked like a log pushing outward. They held the tip of his shaft just snug enough under his testicles. He noticed the elastic trim around his legs followed the contour of the beginnings of the muscle cuts at the base of his balls climbing gently up his inner leg around his sides. Around the back they followed the base of his booty. His penis print was beyond painted on them.

Sean spoke, lovingly, "let me get some of that." He removed a necklaces. Sean ran his index fingers around the bottom of his shorts on his booty to adjust the elastic. He then pinched a little of the fabric on the bottom of his scrotum to pull it somewhat forward. This allowed his swipe to have some more room. When he was done, he instinctively ran three of his fingers on his swipe head to feel the sensation. "I feel heavy. I'm getting thicker." He did it again. "I'm getting hard just being with you." He took his hand to adjust it so it could point upward.

"I want to fuck," Thay said, smiling. Thay stripped slowly in front of him. He noticed Sean's shaft start to push the elastic away from his body.

"Let me see that sexy body." Sean could feel the pleasure of his foreskin start to move off the tip of his penis head. This allow his underwear to rubbed on his head. It brought more sexual delight to Sean's groin. He loved the sensation and anticipation he felt as his meat filled with blood.

Thay kissed him on both his nipples. When Sean embraced him, Thay slipped his finger under his underwear to touch his penis head. He worked Sean's erection up in his underwear. He watched his erection push open the elastic around his waist. "I see you're horny. I am, too." He whispered, aroused at Sean's sexual flush which started to appear.

Sean embraced Thay's naked body hugging him. His hands naturally slide down his back so he could squeeze Thay's ass. "I love how you gently touch me."

"Can we take this into my bedroom." Thay stared at Sean cut body and meat hanging in his fancy underwear. He touch Sean's stomach softly causing more sensation in him. He could sense Sean was growing hornier with each one of his passes. "I don't want Dewayne or Tone to interrupt us. They may be back soon."

Thay checked the lock on the back door that was by the bathroom. He pulled his bedroom doors fully open, it was an older place with two-bedroom doors which slid into the walls. A gentle breeze flowed through the window traveling to Dewayne's room and out his window. "Just leave it open so we get a little breeze." Thay turned on a couple of dim lights to softly lite the room. "I want to see you in your underwear." He sat on the bed stroking and rubbing Sean's groin. "You look so sexy." He placed his other hand on his booty hole to keep arousing him.

"Don't stop," Sean gently replied, popping the top for petroleum jelly container. He watched Thay grabbed a pink device from the draw and a vial of ecstasy. "I want to mate with you."

They both took two drops. Sean watched Thay on the bed, "put some grease on the end of this pink thing." Thay held Sean's hand to grease it with him.

"What is this?" Sean asked, smiling.

"You'll see, my love." Thay smiled. "Spread your legs a little apart." Thay slid his fingers under Sean's shorts to start rubbing grease on his booty hole. He watched Sean's thing hang fully hard.

"Oh, that feels so good," Sean moaned, quietly. "This ecstasy makes me feel so good when I'm having sex with you." He pulled his shorts down in front to release his genital. Sean looked at the device, it looked like a magic marker with a short cord and button connected.

Thay inserted a lubed finger into Sean's hole, then inserted the device and part of the cord.

He moved it up and down inside of Sean.

"F-u-c-k," Sean groan, feeling the sexual gratification it brought. He loved his booty played with, too. He felt a great sexual flush like never before. It started to vibrate in him. The whole area inside his booty suddenly filled his brain with a quenching sexual desire.

He had to grabbed Thay's shoulders because he could barely focus on standing. He felt his inner legs tingle, shooting climactic sensations down to his toes. Precum started flowing out of him. "Fuck, that feels great."

Thay played with Sean's booty hole while he rubbed his testicles. Sean developed a wet spot on his penis head. Thay gently slide his foreskin back and forth. He stared up at Sean, "let me take off these shorts before you cum on them." His brown eyes where so beautiful.

When Thay got Sean's red shorts off, he sat him on the bed. The vibrator was keeping him hard. Thay put some greased-on Sean's swipe. It was so hard it did not lay on his belly, rather it stood in the air above it. "You ain't fuck in a while!"

"No. I took a break knowing you would be out," Sean stated.

"You were saving it for me." Thay began licking the tip of it with his tongue.

"It is so sensitive," Sean rested on his two arm and spread his leg as wide as he could.

He could barely take what Thay was doing to him.

"I'm going to make you feel so good with me," Thay said, feeling his own sensations flow.

Thay climbed on the bed to slide Sean's erection into him. He could feel Sean help with his hands to spread him apart. He kept working himself up and down until his body opened to Sean's large meat. "O…o…o…o," Thay gasped.

When Sean felt Thay's booty slide over it, he let out a loud short moan, "I can't take it. F-u-c-k! I'm so horny right now." His whole groin tingled with the device running in him.

"I see," Thay replied. "I need to ride your trunk, let me feel you explode in me." Thay was rocking slowly taking all of it. Thay started to moan, "I can barely get you in me."

"O-o-h, f-u-c-k," Sean moaned in passion. His need for sex suddenly became stronger than ever. He grabbed Thay so he wouldn't stop.

Thay was groaning heavily, too. "O-o-h, it fills me inside." He watched the expression on Sean's face start to turn to his carnal side. Sean just stared into his eyes holding him so could not get off his swipe.

"Keep to it, Thay," Sean naturally pulled his lips tight showing his teeth. His fleshly, animal side was finally there. The erotic sensations flowed though Sean's brain. His mind closed in on the moment. His climactic feelings started, his brain was screaming for Thay to go faster. His muscles had spasm now and then, he lost all control of his body as his mind was exploding at the intensified carnal desires it brought. "My swipe is pumping all ready, but I haven't not cummed, yet."

Thay kept rocking at the same speed, he felt Sean's body twitch, and his swipe thrust then relax. He knew Sean was having ejaculations. "Big Swipe needs it faster?"

"Y-e-s…, y-e-s." Sean moaned in deep passion. His mind was finally catching up with this new enhance sexual sensation. The sensation was so powerful that Sean could barely think or move, he just laid there gripping Thay. Thay never before road him this slow and gentle. "Make me cream in you."

Thay felt Sean's swipe thrust again. "I can feel you." Thay smiled, then he slowed just a little to prevent Sean from reaching full climax. "I'm gonna make you bust in me like you have never done before." As Thay rode his swipe, he started to moan with each thrust. He started to ooze semen from his penis, it dripped on Sean's belly.

Sean sexual sensitivity was thwarted over his body's needs for sexual gratification to ejaculate sperm. The pleasure felt so good. He dropped his hands now and then pulling on the sheet. His body rejected all attempts to change what was occurring. All Sean could do was grabbed the sheet and moan louder. Sean arched his neck back, "ride the elephant's trunk!!!"

Thay felt another ejaculation in his booty. He rode Sean for fifteen minutes. He felt Sean's legs twitch and watched his stomach muscles tighten and relax. Thay brought his knees up and place his elbow on Sean's chest. Sean was moving his legs back and forth to thrust his penis harder into him. "Is Big Swipe feeling good?"

"Fuck dhis swipe, Thay," Sean kept letting out moans, "fuck it like you know how!" Sean watched Thay as he turn around. Thay was now facing away. He felt his meat bend forward as Thay rode it.

"Y-e-a-h; this is what you need," Thay laid his shoulders between Sean's legs so he could jag himself. He rocked faster on Sean's penis, it slid easily now.

"Y-e-s…, y-e-s," Sean's eyes rolled back, he knew Thay was getting ready to cum. When he pulled on himself, his booty would tighten. His mind went into overdrive as he felt Thay's body preparing to ejaculate. Suddenly, Sean let out a moan in perfect pleasure, "O-o-h!" He sat up to grab Thay and lifted his shoulders off the bed to bite his neck.

"B-i-t-e m-e, Big Swipe." Thay was cumming, too. "Bite me like an a-n-i-m-a-l…"

"Take this load," Sean's climax started. He could feel Thay's booty tighten and loosen around his trunk as his ejaculated. "O-o-h, f-u-c-k!" For seven seconds Sean felt the pleasure of his body ejaculated sperm up his shaft and out its head into Thay's booty. When he was done, he looked at Thay still jagging. So he kept thrusting into him as he held him; the feelings in him were lessening.

Finally, they both lay there. Thay's breathing slowed, he shot a few more times. He then laid back on Sean's chest feeling his swipe still in him. "I feel so good right now, Sean."

Sean wrapped his arms around Thay to hold him. He gently bit him, again. "I don't want to let you go, Thay." He felt his swipe soften and naturally slide out.

Thay's hand went between Sean's legs to turn off the vibrator. As he brought it out, he grabbed Sean's nuts for a gentle tug. He then rolled over to lay on Sean's chest. "I don't want you to let me go, either. I want you to fuck me again!"

11. Dewayne and Tone

Now Tone was a new piece to the puzzle. He was assigned to Sean to look over him. Yet, he have motives of his own. He seemed to want to party as much as Sean. If not more. Yet, he also had eyes on Dewayne, he liked his look. Birds of a feather flock together.

* * *

Thay and Sean heard some noise so they both looked out the bedroom door. Tone and Dewayne were watching from the other bedroom. They could see their shadows in the dim light of Dewayne's bedroom. Sean whispered into Thay's ear asking if his friend, Dewayne, liked to watch others have sex. After the answer, Sean got up.

"Where are you going?" Thay asked.

Sean stood in front of him naked, his swipe was hanging long since they just had sex. It again looked like an elephant's trunk. It swung back and forth as he got up. "I got to piss." Sean stepped to the bathroom. He looked into Dewayne's door. "Hey Tone, you off?"

"Yeah, Uncle G is out there tonight, he is working for me."

"Oh okay. I see you both been peeking," Sean left it at that.

"Yeah." Tone smiled.

Dewayne agreed with a smile.

"I see. You liked what you saw? If you are interested, come to the room after a while." Sean noted quietly. "Dewayne, you cool?"

"Yeah. I like watching the elephant's trunk." He smiled at Tone, "I like watching Tone, too."

"Or, maybe something else, Dewayne?" Sean asked, stroking his swipe. "I got to piss."

"Maybe. Let me talk to Tone. Can you fuck again?" Dewayne replied.

"Now, you know better than to ask that! I love sex!"

Dewayne looked at Tone, "can you do me? Again? Foursome?"

Sean entered the bathroom. Thay stepped in naked and took a washcloth to wipe off his body. His booty and nuts needed special attention. Once Sean was done pissing, he wipe him off, too. "Big Swipe has got my cum on him." As Thay wiped, he had a question, "why were you talking to Dewayne and Tone, Sean?"

"Nothing really. Just asked if they liked what they saw."

When Thay and Sean were back in the bedroom, Sean put on his shorts. He watched Thay stare at him as he did this. Sean slid his swipe into the front and properly adjusted everything. "You like these shorts, don't you?"

"Yes, they make you look so sexy."

"Tell me how?"

"Your stomach: you ain't got a six pack, you got more. I love your look. Those bikini underwear fit you perfectly.

The great elephant's trunk hangs perfectly. Your tight nut sack pushes it out. You fill them so well." He watched Sean meat lengthen as he spoke. He watched him put his hand into his sexy short and lift it so it could swell toward his leg. "You should point it the other way." He gently put his hands in Sean's shorts and bent in the other way. "It makes it push out more." Thay giggled.

"You like the swipe hanging thick like that."

"Yes!" Thay touched his penis head on the outside of his shorts, then stoked his shaft; finally running his finger tips on his nut sack. "Let Dewayne and Tone see you are horny! You know they are watching us like live porn. Give them a show! Let them see the dick!" He slipped his gentle fingers into his shorts to pull his foreskin off his head. "Big Swipe need his penis head to show. I can see your horniness, Sean."

Sean moaned deeply, "you touched the bottom of my swipe's head. That is my g-spot. Rub it with a fingertip. I love that shit." Sean shook a little as Thay did it.

"I see the veins of your meat showing in your shorts." He wanted to tease Sean as much as he could to get another pounding. He liked flirting with Sean.

"Good," Sean reached into his overnight bag, "I bought a pair for you."

"You got me a pair, too," Thay smiled, looking at them. "Okay, I will try them on." He got up and put on his hand on Sean waist. He paused, then gently ran his fingers down the grove on leg to his nut sack, he squeezed then softly. His fingers moved across his shaft as he stepped past to dress in the shorts.

"You know it." Sean smiled, then kissed him. "I like you much."

They both stood toward Dewayne's bedroom door. "Hey Dewayne, hey Tone."

"Hey Thay," they both said.

"Sean and I are going to bed. Maybe you would like to watch again or even join us."

* * *

When Thay and Sean awoke, they were lying in the bed enjoying the cool breeze, while watching some porn on the television. Thay now and them would rub Sean's nuts. Sean would moan, then kiss him. Sean would now and then fix Thay's new shorts so his nuts and swipe looked perfect in them. They decided to have some wine.

When they were lying there, Sean would roll on his side. His swipe pushed against Thay's leg. Thay would eventually turn, too. He would push his booty into Sean's swipe. Other times, Thay would notice Sean getting a semi-erect swipe, so he would lay his head on Sean's chest to look at his shorts. His veins penetrated the fabric if it grew erect. Sean would place his hand on Thay's booty to rub it.

Thay was starting to see into the heart of Sean. He now understood what Sean meant when he said that he would get uncontrollable erections. He was happy and felt good. His body would react to this. Sometimes as he got an erection, he was not always wanting to get off. His body was only reacting to his joy. Thay was starting to learn there was a difference.

Suddenly, they both looked at Dewayne and Tone standing in the doorway. Thay was turned on. "We didn't hear you," he said. He put his hand on his penis to hold his erection.

"We have been watching. I like those shorts, Thay!" Dewayne replied.

"Sean got them for me." Thay got up to show out a little. His meat retracted. "They look nice don't they?"

Dewayne smiled with Tone, "yes."

Sean spoke. "Dewayne, take off all your clothes. You, too, Tone." It wasn't that they were fully dressed, they both were in underwear and T-shirts. Sean looked at Tone's full erection. Sean rolled to his side to watch.

Thay noticed Sean was looking so he laid in front of Sean to push his booty against him, "Dewayne, are you and Tone having fun?"

"Yes," he replied. He grabbed Tone's erection, "let me help you with that."

Tone kissed him. "You like the dick?" He teased.

They both stood there naked.

Now, Dewayne had more man hair. It went up his dick to his stomach and chest. At his chest, it almost looked like an arrow pointing to his chin. It went up the center, but only grew around the center. He had larger nipples poking outward. As you know, he was somewhat thinner.

His penis was blacker than his body's tone. It hung straight like a tube, soft it wasn't more than an inch thick and three inches long. He was cut. His head was a little smaller than his shaft. His nuts hung two inches off his body. His swipe hair wasn't all that long, but it did cover his lower body and grew between his legs up his ass crack.

His penis head around the rim didn't matched his body tone, it was lighter. It was more reddish. When he swelled, it grew to eight inches.

His jaw was a little larger, nose broad, and ears were smaller. He had a very clean face and a nice grin. His teeth were perfect. He was low drama like Thay.

Tone, on the other hand, was lighter: chestnut or caramel. His body was more developed. He was not as developed as Sean, but he had a boxed chest and a solid frame. He was also perfectly proportioned with a thirty-inch waist.

Dewayne and Thay had eyes on Tone. This was the first time Thay saw Tone naked. Dewayne noticed Thay was staring. He sat on the bed with him. "He looks pretty good. You know, like an African warrior that can run many miles and take down his prey with his upper body."

Dewayne and Thay giggled together.

Thay responded, "I like how his dick hangs soft. It must be an inch and a half thick. He has a fat dick, can you take that? It's like a straight stick pointing to the left. I can see both his nuts behind it." While Thay was staring, he sometimes licked his lips. He figured when Tone had a full erection, it was eight inches, maybe ten. His baggy nuts hung about the same length as his penis. "He looks like a bull ready to fuck with those baggy nuts!" Thay chuckled lightly.

They all three watched Tone's swipe thicken. He heard what they said. The flesh behind his penis head stretched an inch. His penis head filled. Tone stroked it a few times enjoying the sensation that is sent through his body. He like hearing them talk.

Dewayne commented, "look at it thicken. Look at that thing!" They both giggled.

Dewayne watched Tone's penis gradually lift to the side. "Look at the rim of his head!" Another giggle followed. "I like his body hair!"

Tone chuckled, pulling on his swipe some more. "Enjoying the show? What is this: sex row? Brother got to get examined. Y'all gonna give me an exam before I get to fuck. You want to check with the boss to see if I fit the profile?" Now his swipe was half hard.

Sean chuckled into Thay's ear.

"I hear you back there laughing!" Dewayne responded.

Tone stepped to Dewayne, "don't stop now. You can start by sucking!" He smiled, "I heard you were really good."

"Yes," Dewayne moaned. He inhaled his dick. It's thickness filled his mouth. He slid off the bed onto his knees. He sat back on his legs and spread them apart. This exposed his booty crack. With his mouth, he worked Tone's head like a scientist. He placed his hands on Tone waist rubbing his groan hair. Dewayne could feel Tone's body tense.

Thay got off the bed, "stop for a second." He grabbed his eye dropper. "You both need some ecstasy."

Dewayne agreed, then lit a blunt, "some of this, too. It is medical marijuana! It is from Canada! It is the bomb!" He stared now and then at Tone's penis as he knelt.

They all glanced at Tone's thick swipe hanging half erect. It looked like a long, fat pickle. A pickle never goes limp. It always was straight; it would either lengthened and thickened, or shortened and thin. When it thinned, it pointed down toward the left.

Sean jagged on him a few times to feel it.

Thay gave Dewayne and Tone three drops. Dewayne naturally placed one of his hands on Thay's lower back and the other on Tone's nuts.

Thay turned and looked at Sean. "You need some?"

They all smoked the blunt together. When Dewayne was done smoking, he kept gently working Tone's swipe and nuts, so he would stay erect. When he handed the blunt to Thay, he bumped his ass into Tone. As Thay smoked, Dewayne turned and got busy giving Tone a blowjizzle.

Sean looked at Thay seeing his print on the shorts, "cloth feels good on the end of your pipe, don't it?"

Dewayne's dick swell hard while he was doing Tone. He kept throwing his booty out to wiggle it.

"Big Swipe horny?" Thay asked, occasionally rubbing Dewayne.

Sean grabbed Thay to put him on his knees. "Give me a blowjizzle, too."

Thay loved his force and his gentleness. Thay naturally licked his lips. Thay looked up at Sean, he reached his arm to feel his chest. He played with his nipples. He licked his stomach and swipe hair. "Big Swipe needs more sex." He watched Sean's head slide out of his foreskin.

Thay spread his knees apart feeling Sean's swipe on his face. He took one hand to play with his man hairs. He watched Sean's swipe grow more. He looked up again at Sean staring at him. He thought, Big Swipe needs sex. He grabbed his nut sack in the shorts to tug on them. "I like this! Your veins are showing."

"O-o-h, fuck," Sean moaned. His penis was fully erect. Sean muscles every now and then on his stomach tighten. Bumps started to appear on his chest. He watched Dewayne sucking Tone's swipe. "Tone, we got to switch!" He pushed Tone over by Thay and slipped his swipe into Dewayne's mouth.

As they did it, everyone looked at Tone. His dick was thick, his nuts kept gently bouncing off Thay face. Thay inhaled his nut sack sucking and licking it. He stroked his shaft. Then, he would move up to suck on the fat muscle laying on his face. "He is like a bull," Thay commented, again, "he gonna need more sex, too!"

After a few minutes, Tone grabbed Sean, "we have to switch, again." Tone forced his thick muscle into Dewayne's mouth. "Give me more head! Suck on me!" Tone started to moan, "you want a facial?"

Dewayne smiled, gently holding the area behind the rim of Tone's head with his teeth, "Yeah!" He watched Tone shake as he licked the tip of his head.

"Easy with the teeth," Tone moaned.

"I want one, too." Thay smiled, looking up at Sean. Thay kept tugging on Sean's nuts.

Tone grabbed Dewayne's ears, thrusting his cock deep into his mouth. Eventually, he started rocking with him. Dewayne gagged now and then, but took it. "Yeah, bitch, let me feel that throat!"

Dewayne kept smiling. He said something, but Tone's cock was ginormous in his mouth so it was just slobber.

"Keep sucking, Thay," Sean started moaning. He planted his hand on the back of Thay head grabbing his hair while watching Dewayne. He was at the point of no return. He didn't want it to stop.

"Y-e-a-h," Tone was losing control. He looked at Dewayne arch his neck up, leveling off with Tone's pipe to slide it all in. Dewayne choked again, he could feel it sliding in his throat. Eventually, he had to come up for air. "It's thick," he gasped for a breath. Once he had air, he licked it and sucked some more.

Soon Tone grabbed himself pulling up and down as fast as he could. He looked a Sean watching him. He watched Thay licking and sucking. All his muscles tensed as he saw Dewayne staring up. Tone was about to let loose, he was moaning hard, "Bitch, you want the shit?"

"Yes please," Dewayne said, timidly, "yes please; yes please." He placed one hand on Tone's nut sack gently massaging it.

"O-o-h, o-o-h," Tone's stomach contracted, then loosen. He grabbed Dewayne's hair.

As Sean watched he removed his swipe from Thay's mouth to start working it. He put one hand on Thay's shoulder. He felt Thay put a hand on his booty to rub it. He watched Thay move even closer to Dewayne. "O-o-h fuck," Sean moaned, pounding himself, "I got a load for you!" He was breathing heavy as hell. He lifted one leg to place it on the bed. "Play with my nuts and booty," Sean let out a heavy, hot moan.

Dewayne reached over to pull on Sean's nut sack. He was now playing with both their nuts. "You both can cum on us."

Thay started jagging Dewayne. Dewayne was watching Sean, Thay, and Tone. "You like what you see?"

"Yes." Sean replied, shaking.

Tone turned Dewayne's head, "here you go, bitch…"

Dewayne replied, "Yes please; yes please; yes please."

"A-w-e; a-w-e; ooh," Tone kept moaning. His baggy balls pulled tight and his body shook as he enter climax. "A-w-e, here you go," he sprayed cum on Dewayne nose, forehead, cheeks, and mouth. Then he took his cock to smear it around his face.

Once Sean saw this, it was over for him. He put a hand on Tone's shoulder shooting on Thay's face. He even shot some on Dewayne, "y-e-a-h, you get some, too." When he was done, he grabbed Thay's head with both hands laying his swipe on Thay's face to rub it around. He spread his legs further apart. "Kiss my nuts."

Thay responded.

As Dewayne watched this, he started shooting cum on Tone's leg and the floor. "O-o-h y-e-a-h…"

He grabbed Thay's penis to jag him off. Once Tone was done, he smeared his face on Tone's leg. "You nut like a bull," he whispered.

"Yeah, I do. Lick on Daddy's dick. Clean that shit off me."

* * *

"I'm going to wipe off," Thay said. He noticed Sean was following so he reached out with his hand to grab Sean's swipe while he led the way. "We all have cummed everywhere!"

Tone and Dewayne followed them. Tone grabbed what was left of the blunt and a lighter.

Dewayne kicked on the bathroom exhaust fan.

As Thay wiped off in the mirror, Sean grabbed a second washcloth to wash Thay's booty and back. "We can jump in the shower."

"Here," Tone passed the blunt to Dewayne.

Thay turn around placing the washcloth down to turn the water on. He held the tip of Sean's swipe to squirt soap on it. They both climbed into the shower. He used both of his wet hands to lather the soap. He wrapped one hand around Sean's thick shaft, "how's that feel?"

Sean looked down as he blew smoke out of the shower area. He watched Thay wash his meat, "feels good." He put the blunt to Thay's lips. "Take a pull before the water hits it."

When Thay was done, he passed it to Tone. "Take it before the water hits it." He saw Dewayne sit on the toilet washing Tone's swipe and legs.

When Tone was done with the last hit, he asked Dewayne, "Where do you want me to put this."

Dewayne stood, "in here." When he lifted the toilet seat, he bumped the side of his booty on Tone's leg.

Tone naturally moved a little, but, to the surprise of Dewayne, Tone place his hand on the top of his booty, "got it." His finger slid up and down his crack.

* * *

Thay was done cleaning both Sean and himself. Sean noticed Thay licking his lips and his swipe hardening. Sean placed the towel on the floor and knelt down, "I see you licking your lips." Out of the shower, Sean said, "blowjizzle time." He inhaled Thay.

"O-o-o," Thay felt Sean's mouth on his penis. His erection grew fast, "O-o-h, suck me off, Sean." He felt one of Sean's hand slide up between his legs. He eased his legs apart. "O-o-o; Dewayne, grab that jelly off the shelf." Thay's head went back as he let out another moan. He put a leg on the edge of the tub.

When Dewayne grabbed the grease, he reached past Tone again, bumping his body.

"Here," he popped open the cover. As he watched Sean slide his hand again between Thay's legs, he bumped into Tone, again. "Nice show, hey?" He gently touched Tone's waist with his fingers. "It is a little tight in here for four people."

Then, Dewayne stepped toward Thay. He started rubbing Thay's belly with his fingertips. "You like this," he said, listening to him moan.

Tone joined them. He slid Thay down a little, Sean naturally followed still working his blowjizzle. Tone lifted Thay's leg off the tub to place it on the toilet cover. Tone hugged Thay and kissed his neck.

"O-o-o;" Thay moaned, gently, "you are all sexing me up. I gonna bust."

"Y-e-a-h," Dewayne whispered.

"I need some;" he paused for another moan when Tone kissed on his neck, "Sean, give me your swipe."

Sean quickly laid another towel out on the floor, "turn around to ride the elephant's trunk."

Dewayne let Thay go, he forced Sean's hand off and started blowing him. "Let me get it real hard." He greased Sean's swipe.

Tone held Thay, kissing him.

"O-o-h, I can feel the bull's lips." Thay turned around to sit on Sean. Dewayne guided Sean into him, "give Thay some dick."

"O-o-o, Big Swipe." He reached back with his arms to place then on the floor. Sean grabbed his waist. "F-u-c-k!!!" He started working himself up and down on Sean. "O-o-o, S-e-a-n," Thay screamed.

"Ride the trunk of the elephant," Sean said passionately. "Ride it…!" He helped him ride. "Ride it, baby!"

Tone put one foot on the toilet seat as Thay rocked his body on the trunk. "Here, suck on this," Tone held his hair as he fucked Sean's swipe. He put his dick in his mouth, "suck this shit!"

Dewayne got between Thay's legs holding his dick in his hand so every time Thay rocked on Sean's dick, it would slide up and down in it.

"O-o-o," Thay moaned, "my little ass can't take all this attention. Sex me up good. O-o-o…" He felt Sean starting to thrust his swipe harder into him. "O-o-h, Big Swipe," he yelled, "I'm creaming!"

Tone pulled Thay's hair, straightening his neck. "You wanted to taste the bull." Thay backed off, giving Tone head, "I'm cumming, Dewayne."

Dewayne jagged him as fast as he could. He watched Thay let out a loud moan. "Cum, Thay, let he see you shoot cream everywhere. Get it all out, you take it so well."

"Okay; o-k-a-y," he moaned, busting more. "I take it so well."

12. Breakfast with the Parents

Well the time came when the visit, or sex-fest, was ending. Tone and Sean had their responsibilities which may have brought even more questions for Thay and Dewayne. Mamma Kay did want to see him. Parents seem to always interrupt fun.

* * *

"Hey, morning," Sean greeted Tone and Dewayne in the kitchen. He was wearing his red shorts.

Thay shot past him running his fingertips on his waist. "You two got up early."

"G-dawg will be up here so I got to be ready to give him a break. He was cool and stayed the whole night."

"Oh," Sean stretched. He naturally reached into his shorts to release the pressure of his morning erection. His hand moved his elongated swipe to allow it to ride to the left in his shorts. Sean didn't really pay attention, but everyone else did.

"There are some apples and oranges over there if you want some," Dewayne gestured.

Thay grabbed his usual box of cereal and milk. He watched Sean stretch again. This time he noticed Sean put both his hands on his lower back and lean outward. It forced his penis print to grow. He could tell his foreskin was still back. "Your back a little sore," he giggled.

"Yea, little, just stretching." He stood by the table next to Thay to grab an apple. He scratched his groin again.

Thay reached with his hands to tenderly adjust Sean's shorts around his swipe and nuts. He ran a few fingers along his pipe. "Your penis is thick this morning," he teased.

"Yeah!" Sean smiled, "I need to fuck some more." Sean kissed Thay. "I usually knock one out in the morning when I am by myself. It is a good 'wake-me-up'."

"Oh, do you now," Thay whispered, "you want me to jag you off?" As Sean sat next to him, he reached into his shorts and started to jerk him softly.

Sean felt his hand rub up and down. He whispered, "I think we have time for one!"

Tone got up to go to the sink. Dewayne stared at his boxers, watching his swipe and nuts bounce around. "I got to get dressed." He headed to Dewayne's bed room.

Sean scratched his nuts. Thay worked him longer. His red shorts had a penis print pointing to the left. Then, he helped massage his nut sack. "I might have to work today, I haven't heard from Unck yet."

"Okay," Thay replied. He removed his hand.

"What do you do?" Dewayne asked.

Sean felt Thay's hand softly touch the inside of his leg near his testicles. "I do stuff, that's it." He glanced at Thay eating his cereal. He moved his leg a little.

Tone entered the kitchen. He was dressed in khakis and a T-shirt. He wore two guns under his arms. "Thanks for the breakfast, Dewayne."

Dewayne smiled, looking at his guns, "what do you do for a job?"

"Security work."

"What kind of security work?"

Sean interrupted, "he works for my Unck; that type of security work. Please don't ask anymore."

"O-k-a-y," Dewayne noted Sean's tone. "Have a good day, Tone."

Suddenly, they all got quiet. There was two raps on their back door then one followed. "Who is that?" Thay asked.

"I'll check," Tone replied. "It is probably G-dawg." Tone looked through the peephole. His whole demeanor changed. "Oh shit," he said softly, "Sean, it's your Unck and Miss Kay! Go get dressed!"

"What???" This was all it took. Sean jumped up, "come on, we got to get dressed."

The three of them ran to the back of the place.

* * *

Tone opened the door, "good morning, sir. Hello, Miss Kay. I'm surprised to see you here. It is early."

"Hey, Tone, how are you doing?" I replied. "G-dawg said he gave you a break to shower and eat."

"I'm doing good, sir. I'm getting ready now to relieve G-dawg. He stayed the night."

"He is waiting." I noted something was going on.

Tone noticed my stone-cold stare. "Yes sir. Well, sir, I'll get down there now."

"Everything okay?" Kay asked, stopping him. "You enjoy your night off?"

"Yes. I slept on the couch."

I softly, but sarcastically, stated, "I'll bet you did! Get your jacket on. We are not trying to bring any attention to ourselves."

Kay glanced up, "Whitey stop!"

"All is quiet. I just need to use the bathroom. And, to check on Sean, of course." Tone adjusted his shirt and pants.

"Sure," I mentioned.

"Whitey," Kay commanded.

This was all it took for me, I bowed down. "Well, I'm glad you have this all under control, Tone." Yet, I did have my questions.

Sean stepped into the kitchen. "Hey, Unck, didn't expect to see you here." He hugged me.

"I'll bet you didn't. Thanks for getting dressed. Mama Kay wanted to check in with you. We picked up some food if anyone is hungry."

"I got you a fruit salad," Mama Kay replied to Sean. Dewayne and Thay entered the kitchen.

"Good morning," Dewayne said.

Thay was a little quieter, "hi."

"We kind of ate, Unck," Sean replied, whispering at the table.

"Good," I whispered back, interrupting, "eat again! Mama Kay picked this shit up." I stared him down!

After Mama Kay was done meeting Dewayne and Thay, she came over by Sean to give him a peck on the cheek.

"We are just checking in on our boy. I wanted to be sure you were okay. You are going to have to get back to work. Your uncle needs you."

"Mama Kay, you are embarrassing me!" Sean noted, quietly. "Hey y-all, Mama Kay got us breakfast."

Dewayne noted, "We just ate…"

"Yes, we did Dewayne, but it wasn't enough. Besides, Mama Kay took all this time to buy it," Sean stared at him.

Tone stepped past Dewayne. "Sorry sir, protocol." He checked Thay, then Dewayne. He whispered to Dewayne as he checked him, "eat again, for Sean's sake."

"Yeah, it was light."

"Good," Mama Kay replied, "I will have the fresh fruit salad."

"I love fresh fruit," Dewayne said.

"It is great, Mama Kay," Sean said.

She asked, "Thay, you are not eating?"

"Well, I just eat cereal in the morning."

"I got some," she placed a box on the table, "do you like this?"

"That is my favorite," Thay was surprised she knew. He glanced at Dewayne. They both had that look: How did she know?

"Ahem," I cleared my throat.

Sean immediately looked up, "yeah Unck, what's up."

"Sean? What are you doing here? Where are you going with this? Kal is expecting you in the gym today for exercise and basketball."

"Unck, really? We are gonna do this now. I'm hanging with some friends! I like Thay and Dewayne!"

I felt a kick to the shin from my woman. "Sean, your Uncle is concerned, that's all. Don't get lost, okay?"

"Unck, why you sweeten me? I told you I like Thay!"

My woman spoke softly, "W-h-i-t-e-y."

"Okay. I need you at work," I politely said.

"Okay, I'll get ready."

"Suited and booted."

"More security work? Right?" He stared at my stone-cold look. "Awe; yes. More security work. A long shift."

"Okay, let me get my stuff."

"We will go out and wait for you. If it is okay, Kay, I'll smoke a cigarette." As I left the apartment, I wondered about the boy. It was different for him. Yet, he was my boy, I wanted him happy!

As we stepped outside, Kay casually turned, "bug the place. We'll watch them all."

"Woman, there something going on! And, tell the kid s-t-o-p spending his money on them two.

* * *

The story ends for now. Sean eventually got back to work. Thay, Dewayne and Sean hung out. Sean wanted Thay to be his house husband. He did his best to stay out of trouble. In time, Sean would go through a moment with them. Eventually, he would push on. What he thought he had was not what he had. Not the picture-perfect story you expected? Troubled times would come. It is what it is.

13. Or, Did the Story Stop?

"W-h-i-t-e-y," the man addressing me had a strange way of dragging out my name, "we need to talk!" He stepped ahead of his group, "you know you don't mess with us Irish folk."

"Is this a parley? O'Neil? You called me to come. You knew I would. What are you saying; what are you telling me? Parley?"

Both our sides were drawing a line. We were all armed to do damage. O'Neil quickly shot me in my vest. He was known to carry a 22-caliber. I fell back on the hood of the family Escalade. All guns went up.

"O'Neil," I yelled, surprised as hell, "you shot me! Why?" I took a breath. "We both have our guns up! Is this what you want?" I stood again.

"W-h-i-t-e-y, that was to get your attention!" He put the pistol back into his pocket. "The rules, Whitey; your family touches one of mine, I reach out. Besides; I know you wear a vest!"

"My family? What?"

O'Neil interrupted, "that laddie." He nodded his head toward Sean.

"What?" I coldly stared at the kid.

"You don't even know, do ya?" He shot me again in the vest, "that's for being a poor Father!"

"D-A-M-M-I-T, O'NEIL! STOP SHOOTING ME!" I stepped toward Sean to brace myself from the shot.

"Don't ya try to hide behind him, W-h-i-t-e-y."

Before he could finish, I ran my hand under Sean's hoodie and slipped an extra gun out of the back of his pants. The gun had a silencer on it so the bullet whistled out. I shot O'Neil in his vest.

O'Neil staggered back, grabbing the hood of his car. He was a feisty one. His main two men moved next to him. "Oh, you're a fast laddie! Didn't see that coming." He caught his breath as he stood again, "Boys, meet W-h-i-t-e-y. They call him Dullahan! The one who rides the black horse."

"Unck, I think he just called you the Street Reaper," Sean said slowly and quietly.

"Yeah…"

"W-h-i-t-e-y, I seem also be missing a flatfoot. Maybe he," O'Neil gestured toward Sean, "could enlighten me?"

* * *

And, the story continues…